PRAISE FOR M. L. BUCHMAN

3x "Top 10 Romance of the Year"

— BOOKLIST

13 times "Top Pick of the Month"

— NIGHT OWL REVIEWS

I became completely immersed in this story and it had me at page one. Entertaining and full of emotion.

— FRESH FICTION, *WHERE DREAMS ARE BORN*

A delightful family drama with a feel good storyline. Readers will relish this entertaining contemporary.

— MIDWEST BOOK REVIEW, *WHERE DREAMS UNFOLD*

A favorite author of mine. I'll read anything that carries his name, no questions asked. Meet your new favorite author!

— THE SASSY BOOKSTER, *FLASH OF FIRE*

M.L. Buchman is guaranteed to get me lost in a good story.

I love Buchman's writing. His vivid descriptions bring everything to life in an unforgettable way.

Buchman has catapulted his way to the top tier of my favorite authors.

The only thing you'll ask yourself is, "When does the next one come out?"

Superb! Miranda is utterly compelling!

Miranda Chase continues to astound and charm.

Escape Rating: A. Five Stars! OMG just start with *Drone* and be prepared for a fantastic binge-read!

WHERE DREAMS ARE WRITTEN

A PIKE PLACE MARKET SEATTLE ROMANCE

M. L. BUCHMAN

Buchman Bookworks

Other works by M. L. Buchman: *(* - also in audio)*

Action-Adventure Thrillers

Dead Chef
One Chef!
Two Chef!

Miranda Chase
Drone*
Thunderbolt*
Condor*
Ghostrider*
Raider*
Chinook*
Havoc*
White Top*

Romantic Suspense

Delta Force
Target Engaged*
Heart Strike*
Wild Justice*
Midnight Trust*

Firehawks
MAIN FLIGHT
Pure Heat
Full Blaze
Hot Point*
Flash of Fire*
Wild Fire
SMOKEJUMPERS
Wildfire at Dawn*
Wildfire at Larch Creek*
Wildfire on the Skagit*

The Night Stalkers
MAIN FLIGHT
The Night Is Mine
I Own the Dawn
Wait Until Dark
Take Over at Midnight

Light Up the Night
Bring On the Dusk
By Break of Day
AND THE NAVY
Christmas at Steel Beach
Christmas at Peleliu Cove
WHITE HOUSE HOLIDAY
Daniel's Christmas*
Frank's Independence Day*
Peter's Christmas*
Zachary's Christmas*
Roy's Independence Day*
Damien's Christmas*
5E
Target of the Heart
Target Lock on Love
Target of Mine
Target of One's Own

Shadow Force: Psi
At the Slightest Sound*
At the Quietest Word*
At the Merest Glance*
At the Clearest Sensation*

White House Protection Force
Off the Leash*
On Your Mark*
In the Weeds*

Contemporary Romance

Eagle Cove
Return to Eagle Cove
Recipe for Eagle Cove
Longing for Eagle Cove
Keepsake for Eagle Cove

Henderson's Ranch
Nathan's Big Sky*
Big Sky, Loyal Heart*
Big Sky Dog Whisperer*

Other works by M. L. Buchman:

Contemporary Romance (cont)

Love Abroad
Heart of the Cotswolds: England
Path of Love: Cinque Terre, Italy

Where Dreams
Where Dreams are Born
Where Dreams Reside
Where Dreams Are of Christmas*
Where Dreams Unfold
Where Dreams Are Written
Where Dreams Continue

Science Fiction / Fantasy

Deities Anonymous
Cookbook from Hell: Reheated
Saviors 101

Single Titles
The Nara Reaction
Monk's Maze
the Me and Elsie Chronicles

Non-Fiction

Strategies for Success
Managing Your Inner Artist/Writer
Estate Planning for Authors*
Character Voice
*Narrate and Record Your Own
Audiobook**

Short Story Series by M. L. Buchman:

Romantic Suspense

Antarctic Ice Fliers

Delta Force
Th Delta Force Shooters
The Delta Force Warriors

Firehawks
The Firehawks Lookouts
The Firehawks Hotshots
The Firebirds

The Night Stalkers
The Night Stalkers 5D Stories
The Night Stalkers 5E Stories
The Night Stalkers CSAR
The Night Stalkers Wedding Stories

US Coast Guard

White House Protection Force

Contemporary Romance

Eagle Cove

Henderson's Ranch*

Where Dreams

Action-Adventure Thrillers

Dead Chef

Miranda Chase Origin Stories

Science Fiction / Fantasy

Deities Anonymous

Other
The Future Night Stalkers
Single Titles

ABOUT THIS TITLE

One broken heart and another never brought to life meet where fashion and fiction merge.

__Josh Harper__, one of the nation's top food writers, had it all — until his life's plot took an unexpected twist. Embracing the challenge, he quits his job and moves to Seattle to pursue his lifelong dream of writing a foodie mystery novel.

With a past hidden behind perfect poise and a studied French accent, __Melanie__ nailed her first swimsuit cover at eighteen. Her super-model career never faltered once — until now. Losing her first job in a decade, she sees the writing on the runway, and it's not the walk she'd planned.

Only together can they write their own happy ending Where Dreams Are Written.

CHAPTER 1

$\mathcal{M}$elanie stood, poised, at the edge of the "wedoption" of her friend Perrin. The ceremony had tradition, spontaneity, and so much heart. A wild mix, just as Perrin was. She had taken vows with her husband as his two children stood by them in Angelo's Tuscan Hearth Ristorante in the heart of Seattle's Pike Place Market.

It was Perrin's new ten-year old son who had named the ceremony. The wedding of Perrin and his dad, and her adoption of Bill's children—the "wedoption." The kids were adopting Perrin as much as she was doing so for them.

It was all so sweet that Melanie felt mushy and sniffly inside, not that she'd ever let it show. She pulled out no handkerchief, had no pockets in her sleek dress to carry one. She only showed emotions carefully, and never mushy and sniffly ones. Being one of the fashion industry's leading models, she'd learned long ago that showing her own emotions was almost never appropriate. Everything she presented, both on the runway and off, was very carefully considered. She occasionally wished she could simply react, but that never seemed to work out.

She let her present boyfriend, Carlo, swirl her into a dance across the space cleared at the middle of the restaurant.

"That was *magnifico*, Carlo. Your *Ave Maria*." The operatic tenor, just finished with a phenomenally successful production at Emerald City Opera, had indeed filled the restaurant with liquid soaring tones that evoked the sanctity of a small church set in the Italian countryside rather than Angelo's fine dining restaurant in the Market.

"This place and Angelo's food made it simple. It looks and smells so Italian. I sing from heart. The couple..." he slipped his hand from her waist for a moment to toss a kiss to the sky.

"Yes, *molto bello*." Melanie had dressed carefully, to not outshine the bride, but she needn't have worried. One of the most innovative designers working today, Perrin had judged herself and her maid-of-honor daughter perfectly despite their sharply contrasting coloring. Perrin's golden hair and fair skin and Tamara's darkly flowing curls and her birth-mother's dusky complexion had both radiated in Perrin's designs.

"I could marriage her myself. So pretty." Carlo swirled her among the other dancers with effortless control. Carlo's French was as poor as her Italian and his English was non-existent. So, she always spoke in her school-girl Italian and he spoke to her in a child's rudimentary French. That way they always understood one another and the inability to discuss more complex topics had not been a major issue. Carlo was not a deep man.

But he was a kind and considerate lover. Also, his Mediterranean-dark skin, classic Italian good looks, and international fame had made them a stunning couple, frequently gracing the tabloid covers. But his limitations had soon become apparent and were now wearying. Soon they would be finished.

"I have received call on phone," he whispered as they pulled together for a slow passage of the song. "Marko Lerano has taken ill and they need an Alfredo for *Traviata* at La Scala."

"That's such wonderful news for you. La Scala," at least she thought it might be, so she offered her support. "When do they need you?"

"I have already called the taxi. They say the tickets at the airport will be. You keep hotel room as long as like."

Well, that was abrupt, but she knew such contracts were rare, vital to a career, and lucrative. Still…

"There is more, isn't there, Carlo?"

He nodded sadly.

She needed no other cue; she was about to be dumped. People didn't dump Melanie, she dumped them. She considered getting angry, but she wasn't, and hated people who put on a show for others. This was the perfect opportunity for a drama queen: a large audience, grinding someone else's celebration to a total, upstaged halt. Why did some women do that? She'd never understood.

What she did know was that, being Italian and male, it would be hard for Carlo to say the next sentence. They had done well together but she too had known it was over, for her at least. She wouldn't have minded if he had been left to pine away for her *un petite moment*, but if such was not to be, *c'est la vie*. She could at least be kind.

"It was a good run, Carlo, *oui?*"

"*Si.*" His appreciation shone on his face and the sagging relief in his shoulders. He kissed her on each cheek. "You are wonderful woman, Melanie. Never let persons tell you not."

"You're wonderful as well," she patted his cheek.

He leaned in for a final kiss, but if they were done, they were done. He was wise enough to hesitate then to pull back and nod. And just that easily, their six months was over. Moments later he had led her gracefully to the edge of the dance floor, offered a final bow, and, after offering congratulations to the groom once more, slipped quietly out of the restaurant.

She stood pillar-still at the edge of the room as dancers

swirled about the dining room floor. Those still at the tables shared stories and smiles among candlelight and buffet dishes.

Melanie sought inside herself for pain, or relief. And found neither. Merely irritation that she had been dumped. The Ice Queen they often called her, due to that perfect mix of self-composure and immense sexuality she could project. It had earned her so many accolades: four swimsuit covers among dozens of others, Victoria's Secret signature model, and ever-increasing offers of obscene amounts of money from *Playboy* that she kept refusing.

Melanie didn't need the money and would never pose nude. She had caused two major photographers to be fired for taking candid shots while she was changing clothes during a shoot; her contract was extremely strict on that point. She wore sheer and skimpy, posed naturally with a well-placed arm and little else, or wore only a Godiva of her trademark waist-length blonde hair. But that's where she drew the line. The stories of those high-profile firings had ensured that all her photographers were particularly careful around her. Neither of those images had made it out of the studio; the second one she'd had to shatter a five-thousand-dollar camera in order to make her point. But it had been made and no one in the industry was likely to forget it.

It was *Playboy's* first offer years before that had led to the final fight, of so many, with her mother. She had taught her daughter many lessons. Melanie had discarded most of them, but two lessons she took to heart: care with her money, and only the work mattered. The professional standards and practices Melanie had worked out on her own.

Carlo had left her by two towering vases filled with lilac and rhododendron, not far from the front door; the flowers nicely accented her maroon dress. She could easily slip away, but found herself unusually reluctant to do so. Melanie never stayed until the end of a party—it might look too desperate—but she remained despite that.

People came and greeted her and were greeted in return, having no idea that for only the second time in her life she had been dropped by a lover. She could forgive Russell because he hadn't known that's what he was doing at the time. Carlo, however, was a sign. Of what? That things were changing?

Jo, one of Perrin's best friends, and her husband Angelo dropped by.

"So glad you could attend," Jo's touch was friendly as they traded cheek-to-cheek kisses. It really touched her and she let her façade melt enough to let them know it. Angelo was Russell's best friend and knew of their failed relationship all too well. And Jo, the calm, cool clear-thinking powerhouse lawyer who now managed the Pike Place Market. Of all the people she knew perhaps Jo was the only one who didn't judge her as anything more than who she was—inside.

"The food. Angelo. Holy *Merde!*" Melanie flapped her hands as if she couldn't think of enough to say. And she couldn't; his cooking really was that good. Yet another reason she was still standing on the far side of the room from the banquet table. He was one of the best Italian chefs in the country and she'd already had too much to eat, but would eat more if she happened to pass too near the sumptuous table.

He positively beamed.

How odd that she and Jo knew each other so little, but knew each other so well. They had cemented their relationship in an airport bar over two photographs, both by the same photographer. One photo, the moment she had fallen in love with Russell as he captured an image he didn't understand; the other of the same moment for Jo and Angelo, though they hadn't yet known.

She and Jo didn't need to speak to recall the moment where they had set the photographs side by side and Jo's life had changed as she saw the images of herself with her future husband. Jo simply held her hands a moment longer and pressed their cheeks together, no air kisses, no need for whispered words, just understanding and acceptance—both rare items in Melanie's world.

The couple moved on but Melanie felt a better than before they'd arrived.

She took a glass of champagne from a passing waiter so that her hands would have something to do. She didn't really want any. The merriment that resounded around the crowded dining room brushed by her as lightly as the smell of Angelo's spicy-marinated lamb—that must be wafting out the windows to tease the tourists walking the cobblestones of Pike Place Market this cool May evening.

Perrin, Jo, and Cassidy—friends since college. And Angelo's mother Maria. They were all so close. You could see it in every gesture. What would it be like to have such friends? She watched them, all happily married. Perrin and Bill dancing to a Fleetwood Mac tune that for some reason was causing their children no end of amusement. Jo and Angelo now with Maria, all tasting the latest dish to come from the kitchen. More food. *Impossible.* Cassidy and Russell also moving across the dance floor.

Melanie took a sip of champagne to hide the pang of envy. Russell was so handsome, having just the right kind of roughness to him, and disgustingly wealthy. Though she had been careful and was quite well off herself, so that had been less of a factor. Still, they would have been a perfect couple…for about a year. Whereas he and Cassidy looked quite content enough to be together the rest of their lives. Again, she resisted the sigh of longing.

Marriage and lifetime were not for her. Still, she could envy the group of friends their stable husbands and their close friendship.

While the other three women were starting college together, Melanie had dropped out of high school to pursue her modeling career. By the time they'd graduated, Melanie had nailed her first swimsuit cover and had put out a restraining order against her ex-manager mother ever contacting her again.

That had been the day she'd legally dropped her last name forever—she wanted no ties to her past. When some form had required two names, she became Melanie Melanie. She'd earned her GED through a correspondence course and her business skills through the college of hard knocks and intense study.

Melanie now hid her desperate, New Jersey past behind careful emotional control and a soft French accent acquired from a learn-at-home computer program and perfected on international photo shoots.

Yet Perrin had made her feel included and welcome rather than the supermodel outsider unexpectedly in their midst. And those who Perrin accepted, her friends accepted without question. It was so unlike Melanie's own world where everything was move and countermove, where the only things that mattered were image and your latest contract. The one escape she allowed herself was into novels, everything else she kept focused on her career.

She allowed herself to simply observe the wedding reception crowd packing the restaurant, taking microscopic sips of champagne to portray herself as content with standing alone.

Angelo's Tuscan Hearth was warm with mahogany tables, blues and yellows on the walls and the midnight dark tablecloths. The wall art was all photographs of the old country by Russell. She had never looked as good as when he was the one photographing her—his retirement from fashion photography had been a blow to the industry.

The dance floor had become more crowded in the few minutes since Carlo's departure. The women wore DKNY, Lauren, Armani, and a fair number of innovative Perrin's Glorious Garb designs. Perrin's work stood out, by not suffering from the classic couture problems. Wearing her designs, a woman could walk out the door and not be out of place strolling through Pike Place Market. They would stand out for their beauty or eye-appeal, but these were not runway-only showpieces.

Perrin's fashion design friends, her new husband Bill's Emerald City Opera companions, and both of their personal friends all jostled happily together, mingling one table to the next. It was a joyous event, laughter an ingredient more common than the regional wines or the amazing food. If she knew how, she would swirl down into the crowd and appear to be enjoying herself. But the artifice usually so readily at hand eluded her and she remained, standing among the flowers.

Perrin swirled by in Bill's arms, laughing and shining with joy—a joy she had created in herself, despite her past.

Melanie found that the most surprising thing of all. She had always seen herself as too damaged to find a true relationship, yet Perrin's past had been far worse than hers. Here she was, Perrin outshining them all so effortlessly.

The bride's dress was a conceptual and technical master-piece. The dress, and the complementary one that Tamara wore, emphasized a fairy lightness, a magic that made them both appear to float about the room; both too joyous to touch anything as mundane as the real world. The diaphanous gold over a form-fitting sapphire sheath—like sunset glistening on the ocean. On Tamara's emerging curves and mahogany red hair it modestly promised the woman yet to come.

"Truly, Perrin," Melanie had told her over appetizers, "even in Milan, such work would be valued." It was no less than the truth.

Russell came by, nudged her slightly closer to one of the flower vases and snapped a couple of quick photos. He may have retired from fashion photography, but his skills had grown rather than diminished. Without doing it consciously, she had watched him move through the room, arranging groups but making them look candid.

Jaspar, Perrin's new son, had taken to following Russell around and the two were now consulting on which shots to take and how to set them up. The boy drank it up like a sponge. Russell with children. Melanie put a hand over her heart to stop the pain at the image. He would be such an amazing father even if they were not to be hers.

The shutter clicked again. She stuck her tongue out at Russell, but pulled it back in before he could raise his camera once more. He laughed, then he and his protégé moved on to other subjects.

She felt her phone buzz. Business. She always let the business line through no matter where she was, except during the wedding ceremony itself. Early in her career, jobs were offered, negotiated, and scheduled in the time span of a week. Now, if they didn't reach you immediately, the job could be gone before you called back. This was a text.

There was only one line: *Sorry. Swimsuit cast now set. Maybe next year. Sue.*

This should have been a contract, not a brush off. This should have been a shot at the cover; her chance to tie Elle for the record of five covers. Instead, she wouldn't be in the issue— for the first time in eight years. There had to be a mistake, but no matter how many times she reread the message, it didn't change. She never begged. She was Melanie. The demand for her modeling time was constant and costly. But this one time she texted back to make sure.

Sue answered immediately, *So sorry. If in my hands, you'd be in. S.*

White lie there, Sue was the editor-in-chief and could easily override any underling's decisions, but you never burned bridges in this industry. So, she wrote back a quick *Thanks and looking forward to next year. M.* White lie back.

It happened.

To others.

Not to Melanie. She'd never lost a contract before. Ever. Not since that photographer's cat had scratched her moments before her first big hand-modeling contract when she'd been eleven. The scar had healed long before the memory of her mother's head-wrenching slap for the lack of caution.

Melanie stood on the periphery of the wedding crowd and used all of her control to remain calm. Passive. *Immobile.* She had known it was time to start planning for her next step. She'd seen too many girls fall by the wayside with no backup plan and many, unlike Melanie, had not been careful with their earnings. There was always some seventeen-year-old with perfect skin waiting to be discovered.

But she hadn't been ready for it yet. Tyra had her talk show and acting. Iman had her cosmetics and had married David Bowie. Naomi was still working, though not as often as she'd like, for a variety of reasons. There were whole chains of super-model restaurants, as if the skill in the studio and on the runway somehow translated across industries, which it almost never did. And there was only one Kate in the world, only one Claudia, only one Heidi.

It wasn't the death knell of her career, but people would hear that she'd lost the swimsuit issue. Soon, not this year but probably next, her contracts would start to go down instead of up in both money and frequency. She hadn't worked this hard to become second-rate. Even if Victoria's Secret renewed her as their signature model, the writing was on the wall.

She moved along the edge of the room to find a chair in which to sit, her *équilibre* was not being reliable at the moment.

Russell, of course, chose that moment to emerge from around the gently flickering fireplace and step in front of her.

She sighed and strengthened her shields.

"Wow! You look like you've just been gut-punched, Melanie. What's up?"

Russell. Of course. The one person who could see when she

was upset. Kind, frequently oblivious, and married to Cassidy Knowles instead of to herself. Russell didn't know everything about her but he knew more than anyone else ever had. Ever. Including how to read the Ice Queen's true emotions if her guard had slipped in the slightest.

There was a time that hadn't been true, but her single failure at making their relationship a lasting one had changed everything, and now he could read her when no others understood. She had been the one to make the mistake of falling in love with him; he had been the one to not notice and leave her behind.

"I appear to have just lost my boyfriend and the next swimsuit issue in the same ten minutes." The shock of saying it aloud cut her inside, despite wearing her cloak of calm for the rest of the world.

"Carlo dumped you? Where is that shit? I'll kick his damned ass for being so stupid." Russell was tall, taller than she was if she hadn't been wearing heels, and began scanning the crowd looking for him.

"Already on his way to Italy, I fear."

"Does he have any idea what he just threw away? Asshole." He sounded truly pissed on her behalf.

Melanie smiled to herself. Although Russell had done the same to her, worse because she'd been in love with him as she'd never been with Carlo di Stefano, he was ready to leap to her defense. She pulled Russell close for just a moment, to share an instant of his strength, then kiss him on the cheek.

"Hey, no falling for my husband." Cassidy came over to join them, she said it with a smile.

"*Excusez-moi.* Too late." Melanie could have bitten off her own tongue. Not that it was a secret, for Melanie had told Jo and whatever one of the three friends knew, they all knew. But the truth behind her words shifted her light joke over closer to envy.

Cassidy's gentle hand of sympathy on Melanie's arm made it

both better and worse. The understanding was kind though, and Cassidy was always kind to the very core.

"What's going on that's made Russell so angry?"

Melanie told her.

"You lost the swimsuit contract?" Cassidy sounded deeply shocked on Melanie's behalf. She at least understood which bit of news was actually important.

"Wait," Russell spun to face her from his continued search for the departed Carlo. "You what? Crap! Is Sue even dumber than Carlo?" Melanie had met Russell while working on a swimsuit issue, had become a key model for Russell Morgan Inc., and shared his bed for almost a year. "I'll give her a call and—"

"And," Cassidy interrupted his growing tirade, "ruin any chance of her ever working with Sue again. No, Russell." Though she was half a head shorter than Russell and looked even more slender than she was when compared with his broad-shouldered frame, it was clear that Cassidy was indeed the right wife for him. She smoothed out Russell's hair-trigger emotions so effortlessly that neither of them probably noticed. They were that much in sync. Like Perrin and Bill, they were each so much better together than apart. Melanie would have gotten right up in his face and they'd have gone at it.

Once again, Melanie felt the stab of envy. Would she ever find a man to love her that much?

"NOW WHAT THE hell am I supposed to do?"

Silence. No one answered. Because no one was there.

Josh Harper stood at the doorway and listened to the odd quality of his voice echoing about his empty Chelsea condo on New York's Lower West Side. No wife, not anymore according to last week's small sheaf of papers and a court ruling. No lawyer, done and paid off the following day. Not even a realtor, "Just leave the key on the counter. The new owners will be changing the locks tomorrow anyway."

He didn't know anything anymore. The underpinnings of his life had been abruptly pulled when the woman he'd adored had decided she was no longer interested in men, or being married to one. No acrimony. No alimony, their incomes were near enough identical. No hurt, at least on her side, just sadness and apologies and a chaste kiss to end the five happiest years of his life.

With the wondrous and painful insight of perspective, he could now see what she meant, who she really was that neither of them had noticed. But that did nothing to ease the pain. Rather it only added to his sense of feeling foolish. He'd been naïve...or dense...or stupid enough to marry and love a woman who...wanted another woman.

He ran a hand over the Gaggenau cook top where they'd made a thousand meals together, the big double oven that had delivered turkeys and pies to large gatherings of friends. Mostly her friends, he could now see. Mostly women, though she swore that hadn't been conscious.

Josh still couldn't understand the echoing emptiness that had so recently been his cozy home. That had included his wife. Worse, she'd known for over half a year but had delayed telling him because she couldn't figure out how to approach the subject without hurting him.

At least she didn't have a girlfriend yet, she'd always been true to him just as he had to her.

One thing was clear, he needed a fresh start.

A completely fresh start.

And he could afford one. With his half of the money from the sale of the condo and furnishings, added to his half of their savings, he was set for a while. For several years if he was careful.

Josh pulled out his phone as he stood there at the door with his computer bag over his shoulder, his only constant companion. He'd left a dozen or so boxes, mostly cookbooks, with a storage company that would ship them if he ever figured out where they should go. His other belongings hadn't even filled the trunk of his BMW waiting for him downstairs. Perhaps he'd been too severe in shedding his past, but that was done now too.

He hit speed dial on his phone. When Shirene answered, he kept it simple.

"I quit."

"Don't be an idiot, Joshua. You can't. You're my senior editor. Your prose is part of what makes *Gourmet Week* hum."

"You have my four emergency articles already on file in case I was sick or something went wrong. Well, it's gone wrong. Consider them and my unused vacation as my thirty days' notice."

"No, Joshua, my friend. For ten years you've dedicated your life—"

"To reporting about food. And it was fun. But it's not what I set out to do in the beginning. It's not what I want to be doing ten years from now. Call Elric, he'll come aboard happily and do a fine job for you. Give you a fresh viewpoint."

"But Joshua—"

"I'm so done, Shirene."

There was a long silence before she finally responded, "If you ever need a job in the industry, I get your first call?"

"You do."

"Promise?"

"Promise."

"And if you need a friend to talk to, you call me anytime, day or night?"

"You're the best, Shirene." A friend to talk to. That finally gave him an idea of where he was going. "If you're ever in Seattle, give a shout."

"Seattle? What the hell's in Seattle?" Spoken like a true New York publisher.

"Me. Bye." Josh hung up, tossed the keys on the counter, and closed the door behind him without looking back.

"Josh, buddy! What the hell are you doing here?"

Josh had chosen a quiet corner in his favorite restaurant, Angelo's Tuscan Hearth Ristorante in Seattle.

"Eating lunch? How about you?"

"Cooking it. Rush is over now, so I'm taking a break before we switch over to dinner prep." Angelo scanned the last few occupied tables and dropped dramatically into the opposite chair as if totally wrecked with exhaustion, which he belied a moment later by sitting up quickly and asking, "Why didn't you come in the back?"

Graziella, the pretty woman who ran front of house, had suggested the same.

Josh shrugged. He'd wanted to just sit. For two years he'd been coming here each time he was in the city. He'd seen it when it was a typical upscale restaurant, and again after Angelo and Russell had transformed it into a Tuscan hearthside with gas fireplaces, understated décor, and Russell's photography of cliff-side vineyards and quiet donkey-wide Italian streets. Angelo's cooking had been the only other element needed to rocket the place into the restaurant firmament. His own reviews had been a part of that process.

"Just wanted to sit and enjoy this wonderful place you've built." Tomorrow he'd start his novel. He was gambling his life savings on his ability to pull it off. But he'd give himself one day to just sit in a corner and pretend that he belonged somewhere. Maybe he could pretend, at least to himself, that he was here to review the restaurant like old times.

Old times.

One of the last four articles he'd kept on file with Shirene was a fresh take on this one chef's influence on the entire country's standard for Italian-American cuisine and the impossibly high bar Angelo had raised. He'd titled it "The Gauntlet" for the challenge of excellence and creativity that Angelo had thrown down before all other chefs. It was probably coming out this week.

"So, how long you in town?" Angelo signaled Graziella as she swept by and asked her for a bowl of pasta. "Long enough for me to roust the others for a meal? Might take a bit, you missed a hell of a wedding party I threw night before last for Perrin and Bill."

Josh actually felt the world spin. It was a little disorienting. In the past he would be in Seattle for just twenty-four to forty-eight hours with *Gourmet Week's* corporate travel department making the travel and hotel arrangements. He never stayed longer because he always wanted to get back to his wife. His ex-wife. Now *his* car, not some rental, was parked three blocks away with all of his life stuffed into it.

"Uh, sure, long enough to arrange a meal. Anytime. This week. Next. Whatever." He knew he wasn't making a lot of sense, but ten days ago he'd still been in a Chelsea condo on Manhattan's Lower West Side. Now, he didn't even know where he'd be sleeping tonight.

Angelo looked at him a bit strangely.

"Hey Angelo," Russell barged in through the kitchen door carrying a bowl of pasta. The last patrons startled under the abrupt assault of his big, deep voice. "Josh! When did you get in? Missed a hell of a wedding."

"I already told him."

Russell dragged over a chair from another table and sat on it backwards. He took a big forkful of the pasta that had probably been for Angelo. Angelo didn't look the least surprised, he just waved a hand at Graziella as she came out of the kitchen and then indicated Russell eating his pasta. She rolled her eyes and doubled back into the kitchen.

Josh realized that he hadn't done much damage to his own serving though he'd been sitting here for some time. He took a forkful, but didn't really taste it.

"I took photos of the wedding buffet for you," Russell spoke around his food with the skill of much practice. "You know, in case you wanted to do a write-up but were too late to see it all pretty. But you never showed. You did RSVP, didn't you?" He turned to Angelo, "He did, didn't he?"

"He did." They both turned accusing gazes upon him, as if he hadn't been busy losing his mind all month.

"I'm not with *Gourmet Week* anymore." Okay, there was something he certainly hadn't intended to say out loud anytime soon. It still surprised him.

"Crap, Angelo. There goes one of your biggest fans. Now we're going to have to break in someone new."

Angelo just shrugged. "So, who are you writing for now?"

"No one." He couldn't breathe; it felt like he'd just jumped off a cliff into nothingness. It was supposed to get easier to say these kind of things.

"God damn it!" Russell almost choked on his spaghetti and booming exclamation combined.

Angelo and Josh both glanced around the dining room, but the last of the midday patrons were gone.

"Did they fire you? Jerks. There's way too much of that going around."

Angelo shrugged when Josh glanced at him for clarification.

"No," Josh paused as Graziella came up.

She set another bowl of pasta in front of Angelo and smacked Russell on the back of the head which only made him smile.

"I quit."

Graziella had been headed away, but stopped and turned back to look at him.

"Fed up with it?" Russell grinned at his own pun. "Food reviewing gone sour?" He clearly thought he was on a roll.

"Something like that." The bitterness on his tongue only supported Russell's teasing.

Angelo and Russell nodded as if that explained everything, which was fine with him. There was plenty of explaining he'd rather not do.

Graziella on the other hand, looked immensely sad. She held up her ring-clad left hand for a moment out of sight of the two guys. It took him a moment to realize that she'd noted the white tan line on his ring finger.

He jerked his own left hand under the table, he still felt naked without the simple circle of gold.

She rested her hand over her heart for a moment and looked incredibly sympathetic. He had told her on his last visit about his wife and how much he loved Constance. He and Graziella had been seated side-by-side the last time he'd been out for a meal and he'd stayed to close the place.

Then she walked up behind Angelo and Russell, smacked them both on the back of their heads at the same time, before returning to other tasks.

While the two guys rubbed their heads and looked after her curiously, Josh did feel rather better.

CHAPTER 2

*M*elanie sat in Perrin's design studio because, sadly, she had nowhere better to be early on a Wednesday afternoon.

It was soothing to at least be surrounded by the process of fashion design: her high stool at the green rubber cutting mat-topped table, the sewing machines lined up along the wall, the wall of cubby holes filled with hundreds of fabrics all neatly folded and organized by the rainbow, the bright steel rolling rack of designs in progress, and the small changing area behind a gaudy Victorian screen. Even the designer sitting across from her doodling away at her sketchpad made it feel so normal when her world was so impossibly not.

Perrin looked elegant, she always did. No matter how crazy her designs, the tall slender blonde made her clothes look exquisite and sexy. And Melanie had not missed that the two of them looked enough alike that what looked enticing on Perrin looked good on her as well. Melanie had a bit more chest and a couple of inches in height, but they were much the same. She'd worn a number of Perrin's pieces that had garnered attention, including the fabulous gown for the opening night of Carlo's opera just four weeks before.

Perrin looked far better than Melanie felt. Dressed in a French peasant blouse, a modern-sleek skirt, and mid-heel sandals, she looked so alive and youthful. In that outfit she shouldn't, but she did. Was it the simple headband the same color as the skirt? Or the contrast of the styles? Melanie wasn't sure. But this look that no designer in their right mind would put together was light and fresh.

"You would have made a good model, Perrin."

Perrin vibrated with a vivacity that would play well on the runway.

"No. As much as I enjoy being a spectacle sometimes, I actually don't enjoy being in front of crowds like that. I like to grab their attention at a restaurant or on the street, but what you do..." she made a mock-shiver with her shoulders, "I'll leave that to someone else."

Melanie had always liked the runway. Enjoyed knowing that she could absolutely command the space so that viewers were dazzled and unable to look elsewhere. Some walkers felt they should be merely perfect "hangers" for the clothes they were paid to display. Melanie didn't agree. It was her job to make a designer look so exceptional that the show ended with people lined up to place orders.

"I like that *énergie* of throwing myself into the walk. It is the magic of a twenty-second declaration of power and control. There, I can unleash that which I must hold under such careful control in the rest of my life." Though she was grateful that she had no show at the moment. Or a shoot. One of the reasons she was so marketable was that she could take that twenty-second runway energy and provide it on demand throughout an eight-hour session in front of the camera. Right now, she didn't know if she could even bring that energy up for a candid.

She felt as if she never would again. As if... The next images were so morose that Melanie really needed a subject change. The last thing she wanted was to impose on her friend.

"You know to throw me out if I'm in your way?"

"Why would I ever do that? You're always welcome here. Actually, I'd love to work on some designs with you again. That dress we made for you for the opera opening, that was so much fun."

"It was," Melanie agreed. Perrin had made her the smash of the opening. And, in turn, Russell made sure that the dress received national attention as part of his marketing support for the opera and for Perrin.

"Besides, you aren't bothering me at all." Perrin began drawing a sketch of something that might have been a large hamster. "I just can't focus to save my life. I never thought I'd be married at all; not really. Always figured I'd find a way to screw up any relationship before it really stood a chance. Now, suddenly I have a husband, two kids, and a dog. I now can't imagine how I lived without them all these years."

Dog. That's what the sketch was. *"Un peu alarming, n'est-ce pas?"*

"More than a little bit. We're having such a fun time settling in that the kids are almost melting down. And me too. We all just have to keep our head in the game. Bill has one more opera before the summer break. Once it's over and the kids are out of school, then we'll get our honeymoon."

"South of France? A Caribbean island?" Melanie had done many shoots in both and wasn't sure which she'd prefer.

"We were thinking of Disneyland. The kids haven't been in years, not since their mom died, and I've never been. It sounds like fun."

Melanie laughed. She couldn't help herself. Perrin made it sound fun, and, of course, it would be with her involved. She pictured Tamara charging around Disneyland with her brother. And her parents. Melanie had only been a few years older when she landed her first magazine cover. *Teen Vogue* had offered her one great prize in addition to the exposure; it had shifted her thoughts into plotting her escape from her mother. Disneyland. How different their worlds were. How glad she was for Tamara.

"Perhaps I shall stow away in one of your valises."

"Nah, all dark and cramped in there. You wouldn't like it." Perrin's smile made Melanie feel welcome and as if she belonged here. Which she did as much as anywhere. She should be getting out of Carlo's hotel room—she really didn't want to spend another night there—but she had nowhere else to go except back to her apartment in New York. There was nothing to do there either. She'd blocked out a long window of time for the swimsuit issue and now had nothing to take its place. But that didn't mean she should impose.

"I should leave so you can work on something other than a dog coat." Melanie began to rise but Perrin waved her back down.

"I'm interviewing a seamstress in a few minutes anyway, several of them I think. I just can't keep up. Before the success of the opera we were already selling stock far faster than I could sew. And with a family now, it's completely overwhelming. I won't miss sewing the same thing over and over anyway; I'd rather design. But the business side and marketing and every-thing else is so overwhelming I can't think. I'm afraid I'm going to have to give up some control, but I hate doing that."

So did Melanie, yet another thing they had in common.

Melanie enjoyed watching the interview. She started as an observer. But she could see Perrin hit a wall far too soon. So, Melanie asked a question, eliciting Perrin's near-panicked relief. After that, they both ran the interview.

Karissa was smart, quiet, and loved to sew. She knew her own limitations, had tried designing and simply not taken to it, but she loved the feel of a well-crafted garment and appeared to know what that meant. Her interview dress was a piece of immaculate construction of her own doing, but not much imagination.

Melanie too knew her own limitations. She'd only ever loved one thing, the business and process of modeling. Some models enjoyed nothing more than the clothes. Others wanted the fame, going for the bad press with wild flings and parties when they couldn't generate the good press.

She'd tried, in the safe seclusion of her Upper East Side apartment, to both design and sew. The Sudanese supermodel Alek Wek had done just that and created her fabulous line of Wek handbags, one of which sat at Melanie's feet. While Melanie had managed some bit of skill, neither had held her interest nor sparked her imagination.

Perrin was all set to hire Karissa on the spot, but Melanie suggested one last step. Karissa was sent to the fabric racks and then the other end of the big cutting table to reproduce one of Perrin's designs, but in a size four instead of a size two—using no pattern but the dress hanging before her.

Raquel, Perrin's store manager, had lined up four candidates who arrived at half hour intervals. The next two seamstresses didn't make it as far as the sewing test: one due to poor skills, and the other one had irritated them both so much that they'd simply shown him the door. Even Karissa had sighed quietly with relief from her assigned sewing machine when the bombastic East European was gone.

The last one, a young gay man named Clem, arrived in a flamboyant suit that bordered on the ridiculous, jacket lapel points almost up to his ears and Capri-length suit pants in dark pinstripe with white socks and cordovan shoes, but the construction was amazing even if the taste level was a bit bizarre. He landed at the machine beside Karissa to create a size six. In moments they were chatting and teasing each other, despite the competition of the interview.

"Do you need two?" Melanie had taken Perrin aside after she

watched Clem ask for guidance from Karissa and how easily they each gave and took direction.

"I don't know, really. Let's go out front and ask Raquel."

The front of Perrin's shop was such a treat; a 1950s diner of chrome and red leatherette, populated by amazingly well-attired mannequins. Melanie always made a point of spending time here each trip to tour the display booths. Everything had changed once again. Prohibition was back, and she'd added Cotton Club and speakeasy posters to the décor. Glam flapper dresses, updated with modern colors sat next to Zoot suits rethought for women.

The best of it were the two booths at the end where she always did her wedding displays. There, snuggled together, looking as if they were waiting for their ice cream, were the sleek wedding dresses. They had the lace shoulders, sleek profiles, and tea-length hemline of the 1930s, and the elegance of Perrin's Glorious Garb. A mannequin poised as a waitress was shockingly attractive in the demure pink satin that didn't feel the least bit demure.

Melanie forced her attention back to Raquel—a striking and buxom redhead, an exemplar of the tradition of that name. With an admirable efficiency, she laid out the orders. Already there was a two-week wait for dresses and business suits that weren't in stock in a particular size. Wedding dresses were booked for two months out.

Melanie glanced at the store's racks, they'd been sufficiently ravaged that Perrin's Glorious Garb was in danger of becoming a custom-to-order shop with nothing to satisfy the impulse or tourist buyer. When a customer strolled in, they needed to be greeted with an abundance of options. A glory of them. Not the almost painfully thin displays she now had.

"*Deux*," Melanie informed Perrin.

"But that's two salaries."

"You need two."

Raquel nodded agreement then set out a sales chart representing the last four quarters.

Melanie inspected it for several long moments. She'd rarely seen such a growth curve. She shared a look with Raquel and they both laughed.

"I know! I've been telling her."

Melanie turned to Perrin, "You had need of two seamstresses two months ago. How have you been doing this by yourself? You'll need another in a month. They'll pay for themselves twice over based on these orders. Restocking the racks and working on the new designs... *Assurément! Deux.* Let us go and see how it is they do."

Neither was done, Perrin's designs weren't simple. But based on the work so far, and with Melanie's confirming nod, Perrin hired them both on the spot with instructions to return tomorrow and finish the dresses.

When the buoyantly giddy pair had been turned over to Raquel for paperwork and the studio was once again quiet, they dropped onto stools to catch their breath.

Melanie was thrilled. The depression that had skirted close beside her for the last two days, as it always did whenever she contemplated her past, had been driven back down into the depths where it belonged.

As they chatted back and forth, oddly about the coat design for Figaro, Perrin's operatically named Cairn terrier presently asleep in a small doggie bed under the table, Melanie had mentioned her need to get out of the hotel room she'd shared with Carlo.

"Oh, you must stay in town until your next contract. Please Melanie? We'll have so much fun." Perrin had grabbed her phone without awaiting a reply and called Mama Maria.

In an eyeblink, Melanie was a bit befuddled to find herself heading off to check out of the hotel. Maria would meet her in half an hour in Pioneer Square. Angelo had a condo there, at the south end of downtown, that he had lived in before marrying Jo. Maria had, in turn, lived there before marrying and moving in with Hogan.

"See," Perrin had insisted, "maybe it will bring you good luck as well."

Why it was that married people always thought their unmarried friends couldn't help but want what they had? Melanie would like to be married someday. But though her career had stumbled, it was far from over and she had no intention of slowing down anytime soon.

That wasn't the issue. She liked the idea enough to let Perrin sweep her along. Besides, the woman was an unstoppable force anyway so resistance really was pointless. The problem was that she didn't know what was now expected in return. Help with a few interviews didn't balance a pleasant and free accommodation in the heart of Seattle's old town district.

Despite her misgivings, between Perrin, a helpful concierge, and Maria, Melanie soon found herself ensconced in a charming condominium just off Seattle's Pioneer Square. On the seventh floor, it peeked over the present Alaskan Way Viaduct elevated roadway, offering a stunning view of Elliott Bay and the Olympics.

"Imagine the view when they finish the tunnel," Maria had said, "and they take away the ugly Viaduct."

It would be stunning. It would offer a premier view in a premier location. Pioneer Square was the founding site of Seattle. And while it was small and quaint, it felt more like New York than much of the city. The area burst forth with more tiny shops and galleries than Soho. Restaurants and bars were tucked in out-of-the-way corners.

Maria told her that the best bookstore in the city was just two blocks away and had a coffee shop; Melanie would have to be particularly careful there—bookstores were a major hazard to her careful budget. The International District offered a small

Chinatown that guaranteed good eating. If she had to be somewhere in Seattle, this would do nicely.

That the condo sat empty most of the time was apparent by the emptiness of the refrigerator, but Melanie preferred to eat out anyway. She only cooked on rare occasion and then very simply. Fruit and yogurt would cover most of her at-home needs; she could practically live on fresh-made smoothies.

It had rich, oak-wood flooring, a heavy-beamed ceiling—high enough to feel open rather than oppressive, and sunny yellow walls sporting pretty framed pictures of Italy: Tuscany, Liguria, and the Piedmont. The living room furnishing could have been her own, an IKEA selection. She'd never felt the need for more in her own personal space.

The masterpiece of the décor was the kitchen. Everything else was comfortable yet little more. But the corridor kitchen clearly belonged to a chef with its generous space, built-in cutting boards, and fierce-looking stove. It had a large walk-in pantry with northern light that stood mostly empty. The two bedrooms were done prettily. She found them to be cozy and took the one that had clearly been Maria's based on the feminine touches in bedspread and art.

Maria fussed and pampered her in a flood of Italian-laden generosity, which was exceedingly kind and did indeed make Melanie feel welcome. If only she didn't have the constant knee-jerk reaction against every possible form of mothering. But she did, and she had to suppress it hard and often. *Maria is not your mother, don't react. Don't react. Don't react.* And she didn't; at least not on the outside.

Permission to stay at the condo also added another checkmark on the ledger sheet of life; she now clearly owed Maria as surely as she owed Perrin. She had no concept of how she'd ever repay either of them.

"As long as you would be liking, Melanie. We have no plan to sell it. It is so convenient, but for now it sits sad and empty. You fix that for us by making it feel useful. It is all paid for and costs us almost nothing, so it is yours to use. No guilt," she'd waggled a finger before Melanie could protest, forcing her to keep her guilt to herself. "It is obvious, young girl, that you need somewhere to stop and breathe. This is where."

She did turn down an invitation to dinner with Maria and her husband, but carefully accepted the hug Maria offered. Such kindness was so rare and precious. And she simply couldn't bring herself to trust it.

Melanie unpacked into one corner of the generous master closet and the built-in dresser designed properly to accommodate a woman. Men always thought four drawers covered all needs—which was all she needed for her current suitcase-sized wardrobe—but she appreciated the design. She liked this room very much and settled in for a quiet evening. She actually didn't need much dinner, and for some reason she was so exhausted that an energy bar with a cup of tea was all she could really stomach. A luxurious rose-scented bath and she was in bed with a book by eight and asleep by nine.

JOSH PARKED his Beemer in the garage. He grabbed his computer and a pack with some clothes, figured everything else could just wait for tomorrow. At this point he simply needed somewhere to collapse.

This morning he'd woken up six hours and a speeding ticket away in Spokane, after crossing the country in five remarkably long days behind the wheel—the Great Plains went on for bloody ever—without any tickets. *Welcome to Washington.* Some greeting.

He hadn't driven across the whole country since a college road trip when he and two buddies had punched straight through from New York to San Francisco in just fourteen minutes under two days. It was Spring Break so they'd spent five days freezing their asses off on the fog-bound coast and then turned around and hammered back. Clancy had gotten the speeding ticket on that trip.

This evening, Angelo had dragged Josh into the restaurant kitchen for dinner. He'd served a venison and baby squash skewer drowned in a morel mushroom sauce with a slow, spicy heat that built and warmed without burning. It almost made Josh wish he was still working as a food writer so that he could dedicate a whole article to this one dish. Russell had called his wife Cassidy to join them. The three of them had spent a merry evening harassing Angelo and his crew from a side prep table while they made dinner service look like an art form rather than a duty.

Angelo's kitchen was a magazine photo-worthy creation; Josh knew because he'd done a feature article on just that kitchen. At the far end was the patissier station that Angelo's mother Maria ruled over. It was now occupied by the night service chef, but all the prep had been done hours before by Maria.

The friturier hovered over his fryers and the grill master and soup potager remained poised for instant action to Angelo's other side. He anchored the center of the line passing prepared plates to the aboyeur Louisa, who cajoled, pleaded, demanded, and absolutely controlled the final dressing of each plate. She also made sure the timing would have the product hit the tables at its very peak moment of perfection.

Josh had avoided most of the unwanted questions by sticking close to Russell so that Graziella couldn't get him aside. And he kept his left hand out of Cassidy's sight as much as possible. When she finally rolled her eyes at him, he caught on that she'd noticed right away: both the missing ring, and his lack of interest in discussing it. After that he relaxed a little.

He'd stayed through closing and cleanup because of the

company, but now he just needed to sleep. Angelo had insisted that he could stay in the condo for as long as he wanted. It was just sitting empty. Angelo said he'd sell it once the old Alaskan Viaduct roadway had finished coming down which would shoot up the property value.

So tired he could barely stay upright, he let himself in, dumped his computer on the first chair he spotted, and headed for the bedroom, not bothering with a light—there was enough light coming in through the uncovered living room window to steer around large objects. He opened the door to pitch darkness. As he reached for a light switch, a small suitcase slammed him square in the chest.

More due to surprise than the force of impact, he crashed backward to the hardwood floor. Good thing he'd already dumped his computer on the chair.

He had a brief impression of long legs sprinting by as he struggled to catch his breath.

"Who the hell are you?" A woman. Pissed woman. From New Jersey by the accent. Wasn't he in Seattle?

Josh rolled up on one elbow as the light flicked on, temporarily blinding his weary, night-adapted eyes. In between cautious eye blinks and narrow squints, he was offered a sideways view of the legs that had flashed by a moment before. They were even longer than his first impression. Atop them was a faded t-shirt with "Versace" across it in large, scripted letters. He was on the verge of admiring the great stream of tousled blonde hair that covered the woman's face when he focused on her hands.

They were clasped directly in front of her and were aiming a...Taser.

"Whoa!" Josh held his hands palm out.

"Answer the question, you bastard!"

He sat up very slowly, keeping his hands in view. A shake of her head flipped most of the bounty of hair back over her shoulder. He recognized her immediately. You couldn't be anywhere near the print magazine industry and not know Melanie, perhaps not anywhere on the planet. He'd only met her the once, while having lunch with Perrin on his last trip to Seattle a couple months before. He'd been unable to speak a word to the breathtaking beauty.

Normally it was the truly iconic chefs he had trouble speaking with even though interviewing chefs had been part of his job. His first meeting with Eric Ripert had nearly killed him and he was sure that it was only because the man was so old-world civilized that he hadn't declared Josh a complete idiot. It had been a total "fan moment."

But Melanie had been worse than that, so stunning and so impossibly real that he'd become totally awkward despite being happily married, or so he'd thought at the time. He could still remember the way she'd smelled from the moment when she had kissed him gently on the cheek in greeting. He'd planned to laugh with his wife over it, except she'd dropped the divorce bomb on him as soon as he walked back into their condo from that trip. Now he'd better get past being tongue-tied if he didn't want to get zapped.

"Hi, Melanie."

She didn't blink or lower her weapon. Well trained by whoever had been her self-defense instructor.

"We met once. Josh Harper. A friend of Perrin and Cassidy's. Actually Cassidy and Perrin's; I've known Cass years longer. Ever since we both did a review of a gourmet burger place that opened on East Fourteenth." And he was babbling.

The weapon lowered partway. Now rather than being aimed at his face, it was more in line with... He casually brought his knees together though he didn't try getting to his feet.

He had to admire the effects of her rapid breathing on the thin t-shirt that ended teasingly high—high enough to indicate if she wore anything underneath, it didn't include shorts.

"Josh Harper?" It started as a question but ended more as a statement. He also noticed her voice shifting out of New Jersey and into New York. "What are you doing here?"

"Angelo gave me a key. And you?"

"His mother was kind enough to do the same."

Josh did his best to offer a laugh, but she hadn't finished lowering the Taser all the way. "I do wish family members would communicate more, don't you?" After a heartbeat or five had passed and she still hadn't lowered her weapon, he nodded toward her hands.

She finally lowered her aim, sliding the Taser back into a large designer handbag resting on the dining table. "It would certainly have made my heart happier if they had done so. That was not an *agréable* way for waking up."

By the end of the sentence her voice had shifted again, this time to the one he remembered from interviews and their one meeting. A smooth-liquid French accent offered not as a coo, but rather as a gentle mask. And now he knew just what it masked. The New York fit her well, the New Jersey made no sense with who she appeared to be, *the* elite member of the New York social and fashion scene.

He risked climbing to his feet. Damn she was tall. With her barefoot, they were the same height. If he shed his sneakers, she'd be… Josh thought about something else as rapidly as his tired brain would allow.

"Sorry for scaring you. I'll just, uh, go find a hotel. Do you know any around here?" He picked up his pack and did his best not to stare. He'd only ever seen Melanie presented to perfection, both as a model and at that afternoon lunch a few months before.

Here, she stood in a t-shirt with no makeup and her hair mussed, and she was even more astonishing, as if by dropping the French accent she was truly revealed. Breathtaking. It was just as difficult to not stare at her delicate, patrician features as it was to not stare at her legs. The power of those intense blue eyes that so defined her public image were no less powerful in private.

She shook her head, "I arrived here just a few hours ago. I only know the hotels uptown."

They shared a smile. Uptown in Seattle was all of a dozen blocks away, not halfway up Manhattan with clear lines of demarcation for the diverse neighborhoods in between.

"It is late," she glanced around until she found a clock. Past midnight. "You should stay here. There are two bedrooms."

"But—" His throat went dry picturing being in the same apartment with Melanie. This wasn't right. He was...no longer married. *Separate bedrooms, separate doors. Get a grip, Josh.*

"You sure you don't mind? It's been a hell of a long day."

With an elegant wave of her hand she indicated another door. She didn't have that painful thinness that so many models cultivated, she looked incredibly fit, just lean and perfect.

Melanie returned to her own room, wishing him a neutrally pleasant goodnight. She passed close enough that he could just catch the slight rose-scent that must be her soap, warm on the gentle breeze of her passage. Not quite close enough to get past that to the woman who had brushed her cheek against his in a French-style greeting back when he'd been a different man, but still it suited her very well.

He couldn't help but admire her careful knee bend, revealing nothing, to pick up her suitcase from where it had landed after knocking him back. Also the view of her departure. Damn but the woman could walk. And this was flat footed, without really trying. In heels and couture, she was generally acknowledged as the best walker presently working the runways.

Josh stood in the middle of the living room after her door closed, wavering as he did so. Whether that was from the exhaustion, the fall, or seeing her so close, he didn't know.

He headed to the other bedroom, didn't bother with the

light, and simply collapsed onto the bed. Too exhausted to move, kick off his shoes, or reach for the covers; he lay there. He thought about how Constance would laugh when he told her that he was sleeping one thin wall away from one of his short-list women.

They'd had a merry date once as they'd each discussed the five people in the world that they would want a free pass on if they ever had a chance at an affair. Melanie had always topped his personal list ever since he'd seen the model's first-ever cover on his high school girlfriend's *Teen Vogue*. He'd looked into buying the back issue years later, but it was one of the very first issues and quite the collector's item, especially when paired with Melanie's subsequent success; far too expensive for a whim.

Constance had bought it for him for his birthday one year. They'd had a laugh over it, then he'd slipped it back into its archival plastic bag, tossed it in his desk, and forgotten about it. It was now in a box down in his BMW, one of the few gifts he'd kept from her.

Constance had joked that she couldn't argue; should the opportunity ever arise Melanie could easily top her own list. He fell asleep before the irony of that long-ago joke could make him break down completely.

CHAPTER 3

*J*osh woke up to an internal alarm clock, one still located on another coast, and couldn't get back to sleep. He took a quick shower and donned fresh clothes before he slipped into the still-dark living room.

No light under Melanie's door. Of course it was barely five in the morning, no sane person would be awake yet.

By the streetlight's glow still coming through the large west-facing living room windows, he surveyed the space. It was mostly a great room made up of entryway, living, and dining all in one space with a generous kitchen in the corner. For that he had to turn on a light.

The space was practically orgasmic. Angelo's hand was clear here, a kitchen designed from scratch by a chef for a chef. All of the equipment top grade, cutting boards, and a second prep sink all perfectly placed. The solid cabinets of natural oak, the counter space broad, even a marble section for pastries.

Then he discovered the massive pantry. Barren except for one rack which sported an awesome collection of kitchen machines, you could easily move a desk and chair into the space. If he could squeeze in a cot, he could happily live right here next to that kitchen. He already had a couple of ideas of what to cook; there was no way he could live here another day with this kitchen and not play in it. Except this was Melanie's place first. Maybe she'd let him come by and cook.

First thing it needed was coffee. An impressive home espresso machine sat in the corner of the main counter with a grinder standing right beside it, but he had no beans. He checked the freezer. Nope. Besides, the grinding would wake Melanie. And there was no way he could start his First Day, *drum roll please,* of his writing career without his morning boost.

He shut off the light, took his computer in a sling-pack over his shoulder, and tip-toed out the door.

Seattle wasn't quiet at this hour, it was silent. Pioneer Square's bars and restaurants had been vibrating with energy when he'd arrived last night. The warm May weather drawing crowds out onto the streets and the small tables set up outside hip bistros. Couples had wandered the art galleries arm-in-arm and small mobs of overdressed and overly effervescent teens flashed fake IDs at anyone who even pretended any interest.

Now the streets belonged to him and some tall guy going into the back entrance of a building. Based on the brief flash of bright lights and shining stainless steel, it looked to be a homeless shelter's kitchen.

He wandered up First Avenue toward Pike Place Market looking for a place to go, not even the coffee places were open. He checked his watch, still too early for the first chefs to hit the Market's stalls. The air was saltwater fresh, but after the traveling he'd done and the sleep he'd missed, he'd need the air to be highly caffeinated as well if it was going to make any difference.

For ten years he'd been reviewing restaurants and food festivals all around the country. From the Bite of Seattle to the Food & Wine Classic in Aspen to the New Orleans Wine & Food Experience, he'd been to and written about them all. He had a press pass for the Experience next week, but he wouldn't be headed to New Orleans to attend. He could hear people congratulating him on "getting out of the rat race" then shaking their heads sadly as soon as his back was turned. He knew it, for he'd done the same thing himself often enough.

No. A fresh start was better. If he could just find some coffee.

Pioneer Square gave way to a few unrestored blocks that had seen better days sixty or seventy years before, as he walked up First Ave. But then he hit the theaters and condo towers that had sprung up in the last decade. Still not a one of their ground-floor coffee shops was open yet.

As he crossed Marion Street, he looked downhill. The day's first ferries for Bainbridge Island and Bremerton on the far side of Puget Sound were pulling out of the docks, the deck lights blazing as they headed to fetch the first big loads of morning commuters. He'd bet they had coffee on board. The sky was brightening, the stars that had reached through the streetlights were slowly fading away.

Even Pike Place Market at the top of the long First Avenue grade was still silent and unlit. The only vendor up and about was the fishmonger. He and his assistants were already pitching ice into the big display cases preparing for the arrival of the day's catch. Their fish were always the freshest. Angelo or Manuel, the executive chef at his second restaurant, would be here right after the fish arrived to make sure they had the absolute best of the selection.

They traded friendly waves, but Josh felt a little disconnected from the world around him and simply continued along the old brick street lit by the bright "Public Market" sign glowing bright red above the market. The hundreds of other shops were still shuttered.

Then, up Post Alley, he spotted a single light. The back door leading into Angelo's kitchen stood open to the morning air. As he approached, he smelled coffee. Rich coffee. Then he spotted

Maria working over her baked goods, the patissier always had early hours to get the ovens up to temp and the breads exactly right.

Coffee, he could just go begging; he'd need at least a lame excuse. It seemed only right that he should go in and apologize for missing her son's wedding party for Bill and Perrin. Yeah, really lame, but he was desperate.

He barely had time to blink before he was seated across the baking prep station from her with a cup of rich Italian roast and a *cornetto* filled with dark Venchi chocolate still so warm from the oven that the chocolate ran down his chin when he bit into it.

"I ran into Melanie last night."

"Oh, where?" Mama Maria Amelia Avico Parrano Stanford was the short version of Sophia Loren: beautiful, very-nicely figured, and aging splendidly. Josh knew that her son Angelo was at least thirty, but it was difficult to equate that as being possible when observing the flour-spattered beauty working across from him.

"Around midnight. At the apartment," he kept his tone dry.

Maria put her fingertips to her lips but they did nothing to hide her smile.

"It's not funny. The woman nearly Tasered me."

"As she should have. You intruding on her in the middle of the night was not nice, Joshua."

Well, clearly he was going to get no sympathy here. He'd have to try the guys later. But he'd bet it wouldn't work there either. They'd have absolutely no pity for him once they heard just how scantily clad his assailant had been.

Maybe he'd just keep his mouth shut; he had to protect her reputation after all. He sipped the coffee again and felt himself waken a little. By tonight his body would be shifting over to West Coast time.

Maria slid another tray of *cornetti* into the oven before

sitting on a stool across from him. He liked the restaurant's kitchen at this time of day. It was dark outside. The only light came from the single overhead that cast its light on the stainless-steel table, but not beyond. Maria was a shadowy figure except for her hands brightly lit as she tore off a corner of her own *cornetto*.

"You must have loved her very much."

Joshua's coffee cup slipped from his nerveless fingers, the black liquid cutting a dark river across the floured work surface. His attempts to apologize were waved off as Maria wiped the surface and poured him a fresh cup.

At a loss for what else to do, he nodded. He still couldn't see the chink in their marriage. Couldn't find the place where they had gone their separate ways and their love had become a façade. Because it hadn't. Their last night together hadn't been filled with anger and biting words, they had simply sat all night on the couch and held each other and cried. Well, she had cried, he'd still been too numb.

"Well," Mama Maria re-dusted her table and began rolling out the next batch of dough, "it is good that you feel so much."

"So that it hurts this badly?" He sounded angry even to himself.

"So that you could have loved so deeply. Your heart is shattered, but it is not broken. It will heal as long as it continues to feel." She brushed a long curl of deep brown hair, with just the slightest hint of gray, back into the kerchief she wore and began rolling out the next batch of dough with the confidence of decades of practice.

He thought about what she was saying. His heart certainly hurt enough to believe it would never heal. Though it did hurt less than it had two months ago, even a week ago when he'd walked out of the New York condo and pointed his car west. As unimaginable as it seemed, maybe someday the pain would ease enough for him to take a breath without whimpering.

Josh didn't see it happening anytime soon, but just maybe it was possible.

"You are either scary smart or just plain scary, Maria. I'm not sure which."

Her smile was radiant, "When you figure it out, could you let Hogan know? My husband often claims that he would very much like the answer to that question."

"Will do." But he wasn't ready for whatever other insight might be coming his way. "Would it be okay if I went out and worked on my computer in the dining area for a while?"

"Of course, Joshua. If you take the small table to the left of the server's station, that is always the last one we seat. You can sit there right through meals if you want to. Now go, do something to fix your heart; I suggest you spend the day pretending it is fine and work on a task that will distract you. I have breakfast to make and then desserts for today's service. When I have the Pandolce Genovese ready, I will bring you a piece."

He gathered up his computer pack, coffee, and *cornetto* before turning for the swinging doors. Just before he crossed the threshold Maria called out after him.

"And don't give Melanie a thought. These things have a way of taking care of themselves." She'd timed her comment perfectly so that he'd actually have to step out of the dark restaurant and back into the dimly lit kitchen if he wanted to ask what in creation she meant by that.

And of course, the woman—who he'd barely given any thought to at all this morning—once again stood in the forefront of his thoughts. Standing there in a worn, too short t-shirt, watching him with the most amazing eyes in the world.

"HE WAS VERY CUTE," Melanie admitted. Still at something of a loss as to what to do with herself, she'd returned to Perrin's store. She felt some responsibility for helping Perrin choose the two seamstresses and she wanted to follow up on how that was working out. It was too little to repay the kindness of connecting her to the condominium, but it was a deposit on account.

Karissa was faster and Clem was more accurate, they complemented each other well.

"I always liked Josh," Perrin admitted as she sorted through a shipment of fabric. Colorful bolts of mid- to lightweight summer fabrics covered most of the cutting table.

Melanie had ended up at a small desk in the corner that was buried in a storm of untended paperwork. For something to do with her hands, she began sorting and stacking it as they talked.

"I never jumped him though. Happily married and all that." Perrin clearly enjoyed her ability to shock, but such things didn't faze Melanie. Instead she agreed, that was a line that she too would never cross.

"No ring," Melanie had noted that as he'd lain on the floor at her feet. "Just the tan line for one."

Perrin disappeared behind a stack of greens: Lime, Hemlock, Apple, and Loden. "Well, if that's true, something major happened. He was one of those guys who never stopped going on once you got him on the subject of his wife."

"Well, he certainly didn't mention her while I had my Taser aimed at him."

"You aimed a Taser at him?" Perrin popped back up to look at her. She looked like a mischievous modern-day angel wrapped in a tight, over-scale herringbone-print hoodie. "Did you shoot him?"

"*Non!*" She'd never shot anyone except a training mannequin. "Though I came close, he did very much scare me." And then this morning he'd been gone before she'd woken up. No note or anything, not that there was any reason he would leave one. She was nosy enough to peek in the other bedroom and see that his pack was still on the floor and the covers looked as if he'd slept on top of them and then not bothered to straighten it all up afterwards.

Did she like or dislike the implication that he would be returning? She wasn't sure. They would have to talk it over; she wasn't exactly in the mood to cohabit with anyone. Especially not mere days after breaking it off with Carlo. She sighed to herself. After Carlo breaking it off with her. It might be nice to have a man-free zone while she re-gathered her self-esteem.

Perrin turned back to her fabrics, testing the drape and lie of a couple of them.

Melanie focused on the papers before her. There were bills to pay with completed but unsigned checks, probably prepared by Raquel. Good, that meant Perrin wasn't letting others make her payments. Sign your own checks for your own business. None were over seven days old. Also good.

There was a fair wad of fan letters. Melanie was used to these, but was surprised to see that a designer also received them. Most were harmless, only a few creepy ones, and no gross ones; her own mail had the reverse ratios.

There was also a thin stack of general correspondence. She started reading without really thinking about it. Then she read another and a third.

"Perrin?"

"What do you think of this one?" she held up a swatch of Malachite Green.

"Not with your skin, *non*. *En réalité*, I'm not sure any woman could get away with that unless they were going to a costume ball as a harlequin."

"That's what I thought," Perrin tossed it aside and continued her sorting. "Don't know why I ordered it in the first place."

Karissa and Clem were conferring over whether they needed to hand roll the hem. When they decided that was what the fabric called for, Melanie relaxed. They did have a proper sense of what was required to execute Perrin's effortless styles. She was also pleased to note that neither had to ask the other how to execute it.

"Perrin," then Melanie realized that she already had Perrin's attention, the woman was just multi-tasking. "I hope you do not mind that I—"

"If I did, I would have stopped you before you got to the fan mail."

Melanie had only seen a few times how sharp a person Perrin was, in addition to her design work. She wore a cloak of wild craziness that distracted like…ah. It distracted like Melanie's accent. A revelation she'd regretted making to Joshua last night, but he'd scared her all the way down to her core.

Whenever her childhood New Jersey accent slipped back to the fore it made her feel unclean. She'd had to take a shower to scrub it off before she'd been able to go back to bed. Still, she'd lain awake far into the night. She couldn't write it off as adrenaline let-down, her heart rate was unexceptional. It was… She pictured the moment again. How Josh Harper had looked after getting over his surprise. No, not how he'd looked, how he'd looked at her.

She knew that her legs were one of her best features. And while he had obviously noted them, he had spoken neither to her legs nor her breasts. Disconcertingly, he had looked right at her. As if having heard her original, hated voice, he somehow saw the real her. No one did that, not Russell or Perrin. Maybe not even herself. But she suspected that somehow Joshua did.

"Some of that fan mail stuff is pretty weird," Perrin shrugged uncomfortably. "I don't know what to do with it."

Melanie waved at the thick stack of letters, "I send them a signed photo." Except for the creepy and the scary ones. "You should use this pile to create a mailing list. Just give them to Raquel and she can use them to send out your season-line brochures."

Perrin suddenly became deeply absorbed in sorting a stack of reds. She set aside a Persimmon and a Cayenne, not a color combination Melanie would have expected, but she did like the way it felt to her eyes.

She nodded when Perrin sent her a questioning glance.

Taking up the two fabrics side by side, she walked over to the wall of fabrics stacked on shelves down one of the studio's long walls and began holding them up to different fabrics, both complementary and contrasting.

Melanie read between the lines, "You have no season-line brochure."

"I barely have a season-line," was Perrin's whispered response.

Melanie moved up beside her and rested a calming hand on Perrin's arm. She was practically vibrating with nerves.

"Perrin."

This time Perrin looked up at her and Melanie could see the incipient panic so close below the surface. That's when she realized that Perrin's success had already overwhelmed her and now she was losing control.

That also would explain the letters that Melanie had sorted aside from all of the other untended business. Those were requests for major blocks of work. An Off-Broadway show, five society weddings—three of them complete ensembles from mother-of-the-bride on up, even a request from Kate at *Fashion Alive* magazine. She was just a junior editor at the magazine, but she had a discerning eye and was looking to make her mark. She wanted to come for a visit and see a show.

Perrin took one look at the letters in Melanie's other hand and shied away toward a horrid Cyber Yellow that had nothing to do with two reds she was still holding.

Melanie took the letters back to the desk, found a folder and tucked them inside. No wonder they'd been at the bottom of the pile of unfinished business, they were scaring the woman to death.

"Come here," Melanie called her over.

Perrin came, still clutching her two pieces of red fabric and a swatch of the Cyber Yellow.

Melanie knew when a little harsh therapy was needed and pushed her into the chair. She relieved Perrin of the reds with a bit of a tug, secured the yellow with an extra sharp tug, and then put a pen in her hand.

"First, you sign these checks and pay all of your bills. Then we give the bills and the fan mail to Raquel to deal with."

Perrin nodded mechanically and began signing.

"What about the other—" the poor woman couldn't finish the sentence.

"We forget about those and I take you out to lunch."

Perrin didn't protest about the unsorted mounds of fabric awaiting her. She nodded again and worked her way through the bills.

AUBREY JAMES PACED *the tables as if he were inspecting a firing squad rather than judging a cook-off at the county fair. He was a tall, spare man who walked with a pronounced stoop and clenched his hands firmly behind his back. A frock coat and a beaver top hat would have placed him comfortably in the eighteenth century where...*

Josh glared at his laptop's screen, "Where mystery novels go to die." It was his tenth opening just this morning and not a single one had led anywhere. At least this one had the decency to die quickly unlike the three full pages of crap he'd given to Felicity James, clearly Aubrey's evil twin sister.

He reached for his coffee, but it was long gone cold. He took a sip anyway.

Then he looked up in some shock. The restaurant which had

been comfortably dark, only the soft worklight over the server's station lighting the entire space, was now vibrant with light, patrons, noise, and food. His stomach rumbled. Angelo's had filled with a lunch crowd without his consciously noticing. There were chattering tourists, small family groups for whom lunch at Angelo's was obviously a splurge—dinner being out of their reach, and many wearing Seattle-casual who were so underdressed that they were clearly labeled as being very well off.

Thinking back, he could remember hearing things. But he'd been lost in trying to grind out an opening scene to the novel. He'd been meaning to write a foodie mystery since, well, forever. So, despite the miserable openings he'd created, he'd take it as encouraging that he'd become too absorbed to be distracted by what was going on around him.

His was one of the few tables not filled with patrons. *Paying* patrons.

Graziella swung into the server's station to collect some menus to take back to the greeter's station.

"Ah. The writer emerges," her smile lit her beautiful Italian face. Her English had only the slightest trace of an Italian accent. She ruled the front of house with an iron hand, but she added an Italian greeting, a Mediterranean flair for warmth, and utter ease to her seamless service. That the girl was also drop dead gorgeous and glowed with joy anytime you mentioned her chef-husband Manuel, only added to the charming atmosphere she created.

"I guess. Is it okay that I'm—"

"Angelo has declared this table as yours. Most *patroni* paying our prices and eating our food don't want to sit so closely beside the wait staff. We usually only seat our personal guests here. You look hungry, I'll bring you a bowl of chicken skewers marinated overnight in white wine and baked with an Umbrian spice rub served over fresh-made pepper linguine."

He was too busy salivating to protest about not wanting to mooch before she whisked off to greet some new arrivals.

He was again scowling at Aubrey James to see if he was salvageable, when someone joyfully called his name and practically launched herself into his arms.

"Perrin!" he gave her a tight hug. "I'm so sorry I missed your wedding, but—"

She kissed him on the tip of his nose then snagged his left hand.

"But," she said with a sudden, soft sympathy. She rubbed her thumb over the spot where his wedding ring had been and it all slammed back in. Then, with her flawless timing, before he could once again feel all of the gloom of the world crashing down on him, she turned on one of her radiant smiles.

"If only you'd told me sooner, Josh, I wouldn't have fallen in love with Bill and his children. Our children," she corrected herself and her smile bloomed even brighter. "Then I could have been all yours as I always promised. Alas, now we're not meant to be."

Perrin had made any number of flirty passes at him over the couple of years since they'd met. Always harmless fun. She was always an enjoyable woman, who'd have driven him nuts trying to live with that wild energy of hers.

She dropped into a chair and turned to address her companion, "But he'd be perfect for you."

That's when Josh focused beyond Perrin.

Melanie stood there: quiet, self-contained, and breathtaking. In sharp contrast to the last time he'd seen her, she was impeccably dressed. Her long hair pulled back in a tight ponytail, a designer cashmere sweater that draped down to mid-thigh captured at the waist with a wide belt of hand-tooled leather that slid down over one hip like a caress, tight slacks that had clearly been made with her legs in mind. Actually, seeing as this was Melanie—they probably had been designed specifically to be modeled by her. Leather sandals and unpainted nails finished off the delightful picture. He could feel his brain knotting up again and nothing he did seemed to fight it off.

Perrin waved Melanie to join them.

"We do no want to disturb..." Melanie's soft French was firmly in place.

"Oh, yes we do." Perrin pushed the lid of his laptop closed with a sharp snap.

"It was just as well. Aubrey James had been no more interesting than Sheldon Taylor or Percival Cummings or..." he shrugged his apathy, even if his shoulder cramped a little on the way up.

Melanie settled with a grace and poise that Perrin thoroughly lacked. But to see them sitting side by side was actually pretty surprising. Perrin's personality was always so big that it overshadowed her beauty. But side by side with Melanie, the two women could almost be sisters.

Yet there was more to Melanie than looks. She might think she was hiding behind a tall protective wall of French elegance and reserve. But Josh had heard her true accent and seen her streetfighter's stance. There was a strong and tenacious woman in there as well; such a sharp contrast to her outer mien that he had trouble crediting it. But he could see it in her eyes.

He shoved his laptop into his bag and smiled at the two of them. "I'd be thrilled if you two would join me for lunch." He'd also be the envy of every man in the room. He nearly said it aloud, would have if it had been only Perrin, for she'd have been tickled by the idea. But for Melanie, it was probably something she heard far too often, being credited only for her beauty. Well, if that was how she was perceived and treated, he would be the exception to the rule. He'd start with being real.

"I'm so sorry that I scared you last night. 'Course you scared the crap out of *me*; turnabout is fair play, I guess. So, we're kind of even on that. But are you comfortable with me there in the condo? I can find somewhere else to go if you aren't. Though I'd hate to leave that kitchen before I had a chance to try it out."

Melanie studied him and he learned something else about her in that moment. In addition to being beautiful, Melanie was smart. He could see her weighing factors, assessing him, a quick glance to Perrin as if factoring in Perrin's greeting of him.

He now knew that the model's stellar career had been no lucky coincidence of fate and fortunate genes, but rather a success engineered by a highly intelligent woman. Then she offered a smile that knocked him back in his chair, not with its force, but rather its genuine unaffected nature. In a funny way, it made the gorgeous supermodel into a beautiful woman.

"I think it will be *agréable* if you were to remain," Melanie offered and sipped at the water and iced tea that Graziella had somehow spirited to their table with none of them noticing.

He would like very much to know what factors had just been included in her decision.

HAD JOSHUA HARPER done more than a cursory appreciative look at her outfit, or had made some stupid guy comment about "having two tall blondes for lunch," Melanie would have asked him to leave the condo before nightfall.

But he hadn't.

Instead, he'd cut straight to the first thing between them. No comment about last night, no leer because he'd seen her in a state of *déshabillé* that few men ever had. And he'd offered to move out rather than asking if he could stay. Obviously a friend of both Angelo and Perrin, the latter opinion carrying a surprising amount of weight...

Melanie looked again at Perrin in surprise to see if she'd reacted, but she was still doing that cheerful, exuding-joy-at-the-whole-world thing she did so well. She was still the same woman; so whatever had shifted had been inside Melanie. Some part of her had decided to trust Perrin's instincts, beyond the world of fashion and now extending out to people.

She'd decided it would indeed be very agreeable to have Joshua Harper staying there and had told him so. And again surprised herself. It was one thing to think it, but why had she added "nice" to her statement? Perhaps he wouldn't know that *agréable* implied more than the English "agreeable."

This time it was Joshua she turned to assess. She sometimes wished that she could turn it off, step back and simply accept people, but she'd learned to choose even casual acquaintances very carefully as a survival trait. She'd done it for so long now that she could only be amazed that others didn't do the same.

Joshua leaned in to laugh at some tease by Perrin. He was handsome, with softly curling dark hair and a well-defined chin. He had an easy smile. However, just as she'd noted the first time they'd met months before, it was mostly for Perrin.

He began telling her of last night's events and Perrin was listening as if she hadn't already heard it from Melanie. Joshua did leave off the part of how scantily clad Melanie had been, but was entertaining Perrin with a description of his being sprawled at a beautiful woman's feet and facing a fearsome weapon of death as if she'd wielded a machine gun, or perhaps an entire Schwarzenegger-esque arsenal based on his embellishments.

Melanie felt a pinch as she watched him regaling Perrin. Of course Perrin was smiling at him and what was she doing? Remembering from last night that he was as tall as she was, and liking that. Assessing, calculating—gods, she'd shut it off if she could.

His story over, Perrin had asked him what he was working on.

"A novel," then Joshua had blushed.

"How's it going?" Perrin ordered a shrimp *panino* and salad. Melanie selected the same, slightly envying the lush bowl of pasta that Joshua was served. This was her carbs-allowed meal, but pasta was for splurge, not for everyday.

"It sucks!"

Melanie laughed. She didn't know why. It just came out. His clearly conflicted emotions about his book didn't stop his wry humor. She hadn't expected him to be so…unforced.

He looked at her in wonder as if she'd just sung an aria.

She was tempted to snap out "What?" but his smile had answered her laugh. So, she changed her path.

"And why, Mr. Harper, does it suck?"

"Nah," he shook his head. "Been working on it all morning and I'm sick of it. Tell me something from another world. What is amazing and new in the fashion world?"

That easily, he turned the topic away from himself. She began to feel suspicious now—men loved to talk about themselves. No man was that thoughtful, were they? Or had she truly become so calloused and suspicious of everyone's ulterior motives?

Maybe—just while she was in Seattle, which wouldn't be for long anyway—she would try being a different person.

Perrin had begun discussing her new fabrics and some of the textural ideas that were sparking already for her next creations.

Melanie waited. She'd suggested lunch to get Perrin out of her workspace and ready to talk about her business. She'd dismissed the idea when Perrin had chosen to sit with Joshua. But now… He had opened a door out of kind consideration rather than talking about himself. She waited her moment and joined the conversation just as the salad was served with a balsamic vinaigrette on the side.

"The amazing thing, Joshua—"

"Josh."

"*Non.* I will call you Joshua."

The polite bow of his head tickled her. She always called people by their full name to keep them at a distance. With a simple gesture and smile, he had shifted it from a formality to an endearment. So simply that she couldn't help but feel charmed by him.

"The amazing thing, *Joshua*," she smiled back despite her normal practice of reserve, "is the other requests that Perrin's Glorious Garb is receiving."

"It's just letters—" Perrin tried to cut her off.

"Society weddings, an Off-Broadway show. Next, Hollywood will come calling."

"Well, actually..." Perrin was studying her salad. "I got a couple of e-mails, but they scared me." Then she looked up. "Melanie! I can't do what I need for the shop. How can I do the rest of that?"

Before Melanie could begin to explain, Joshua rested a hand on Perrin's arm and drew aside her attention. Melanie wanted to snap at him for interfering.

"The first question, Perrin," he withdrew his hand as the sandwiches arrived. "Is do you want to do those things? I heard you absolutely killed at the opera, but did you enjoy it?"

"Are you kidding?" Perrin waved her *panino* in the air in her sudden excitement. "The chance to build a three-hundred-piece collection was fabulous. Defining the anchoring three styles and fifteen main costumes. And big weddings are just another grand story. If I could only..."

Joshua cut her off with one of his marvelous laughs; Melanie could really get to like that laugh. It made her feel cheerful, though she was irritated with his interruption.

"So, do it!" Joshua told her.

He was right. He had cut directly to the core. Did Perrin even want this? That was the key success factor and she hadn't even thought to bring it up.

Perrin stopped chewing and stared at him. Her body, normally vibrating with energy had suddenly gone still.

"How?" It was barely a whisper.

"Not a clue."

Perrin gasped, swore in a quite unladylike way, then stuck her tongue out at him.

"But," then Joshua turned those warm, dark eyes on Melanie. "I'll bet she knows."

Now it was her turn to be stunned to silence. People only ever learned the hard way that Melanie was a businesswoman first and a model second. She had studied, even paid for two night courses and private tutoring from an attorney to make sure she understood contract law well enough to negotiate her own. Her contracts were the best in the business. She'd seen the crap offered to most other models and, after soliciting Melanie's advice, they took the contracts anyway, which was head-shakingly stupid but sadly unsurprising.

But no one had ever seen that about her until they were on the wrong side of the negotiating table. With Joshua she'd shared two meals and a mutual scare and somehow he saw—

"Do you?" Perrin was asking her. That wide-eyed innocent girl shining through despite her dark past.

Melanie took a bite of her own *panino* to buy herself a moment. Oh, Angelo was so good. The taste of the simple toasted sandwich unfolded in layers. She shook off the invitation to a playful journey that the food attempted to lead her along, and shifted her attention back to the discussion of Perrin's business.

Her friend's talent, work ethic, and dedication to the craft weren't a question. She was one of the most innovative yet effective designers working today. She understood how to elevate both everyday wear and wedding wear without forcing them onto the runway. Melanie herself had worn some of Perrin's styles out on the streets of New York and simply felt fabulous, not out of place.

And she knew how to make a woman look incredible; she really understood the female form. And not just the model thin; she'd seen Rubenesque women shining in Perrin's dresses.

The demand was there as evidenced by Raquel's numbers and the folder of requests resting in Melanie's handbag. And if there were e-mails in addition to those... She began calculating assets. Russell had already done some ads for Perrin—his fashion-photography name still had immense clout in the industry. She'd need—

Melanie pulled back, would have sat back except for the years she'd spent training herself into a perfect posture. It was a fascinating puzzle, but not one she was a part of.

"Do you?" Perrin asked again in the voice of hers that none could deny.

"It's not a small project."

"I get that," suddenly the business side of Perrin was at the table as well. This was a woman Melanie had only glimpsed the once before. "Do you, Melanie, know how to do this?" This was no longer a vague question by a hopeful excited beginner. This was a fellow professional.

"No, I don't," Melanie had to be honest. She'd never taken a design house to market before.

Perrin looked deflated.

Joshua looked at her as if he didn't believe her. He even had a bit of a smile. Then he said, "But..." and left it hanging.

"But," Melanie conceded, "I do know what it would take to figure out."

CHAPTER 4

*H*ours later, Melanie still didn't know why she'd said that. It had unnerved her enough that she hadn't rejoined Perrin at the shop. Instead she'd gone down to Elliot Bay Books at the south end of Pioneer Square, a few blocks past the condo.

As promised, it was a magnificent store, a labyrinthine collection set in interconnected lofty, bright spaces. A little wooden ramp led up to Pacific Northwest history and women's fiction. At the far end of the ramp, bookcases of age-worn wood were crammed to bursting with an excellent humor collection.

In the room beyond ranged a vast collection of science fiction, romances, mystery, and more, simply poised and awaiting their moment to leap from the shelf into a patron's hands. She found new books by two of her favorite mystery authors, and a military romantic suspense that she didn't know but promised a strong heroine. She did enjoy reading about strong women.

She and her stack of books had ended up downstairs in the coffee shop with a pot of peppermint tea and a Bing cherry biscotti—another carb, but at the moment, she needed it. It looked as if Seattle might have been founded in this very room. Age-darkened wood tables, stout but comfortable chairs, and soft lighting perfect for reading and relaxing. Just beyond lay a line of heavy wood pillars supporting the floor above, a large array of chairs and a podium for author readings; she'd need to get a schedule to see if there was anyone interesting in the next few days. And everywhere there were colorfully filled bookcases wrapping the walls and defining spaces.

This was as close to heaven as Melanie had been in a long time. She poured her tea and settled in to choose which book she would read first, and thought of Joshua.

What had the man been writing? A novel, but he'd never said more. She'd never dated a writer; truth be told, she found them a little daunting. Her five new books—she'd managed to cut herself off at five—showed the diversity that could imply. The walls around her only reinforced that there was no way to guess.

Nor could she guess how he had seen through *her* careful walls. No one saw past the supermodel. Jo had only seen the model who had loved Russell. Russell could see something of her emotions, but no matter how protective of her he was— which was quite charming as she really didn't need it, but it was so kind that she let him think so—he saw her only as a celebrity and former lover.

She and Perrin had designed a few dresses together, which had been an exciting and fascinating experience. Perrin's creativity and her own knowledge of the industry had combined to make a truly special gown for the opera's opening. Perrin had also shared Melanie's own need to leave her past behind and start clean, something they'd easily recognized in each other. It made them compatible, but even Perrin didn't see who she really was.

Only Joshua walked right past the supermodel and

addressed Melanie directly. It didn't make sense, but it was the only way she could describe the feeling.

She'd created a career based upon a chance crossing of genetics and an attitude she'd always known how to control and deliver. Those were the tools of the persona that she presented the world, and the world had paid her very handsomely for that. But the money had been paid to the exterior mask, not the woman within.

Her business-side skills, those she had created from scratch through intensely hard work and painful experience. It was the businessperson who felt most like her because she'd earned every single bit of that knowledge on her own.

Joshua had not only seen, but complimented the second woman. No man had ever seen past her beauty, not even Russell.

Instead of settling in with her books, she slipped out the folder of Perrin's letters and read through them more carefully. It was an interesting problem. Design houses were often based upon a single person's genius. It was a matter of developing a support system that both leveraged their skills and isolated them so that they could do whatever it was they did best. The finest designers possessed some kind of synaptic connections that were as unique as her own genes.

Designers could be wildcards like Karan, eccentrics like the reclusive Zoran, or born marketers like Hilfiger. They could lead their own companies, for better or worse, or turn it over to a CEO who understood and worked with them.

It was the shoestring years that were the problem. Perrin was trying to add the occasional seamstress, but she'd need to have a great deal of preparation in place to handle the requests now spread across the bookstore table. She'd been right to be afraid of these, but the opportunity sizzled in Melanie's fingers it was so hot. She could feel the potential radiating off them.

Melanie left her tea for a moment to return upstairs and

purchase an attractive, leather-bound journal she'd spotted earlier by the cash register. Back to her book-lined corner downstairs, she began sketching out just what it might take for Perrin's Glorious Garb to climb the next level. Her tea was long gone cold by the time she remembered it.

JOSH HAD SPENT the afternoon doing a market run to stock the kitchen. There was nothing like Pike Place Market in New York City. The produce here should be on cooking shows, not sitting out for purchase. The freshness and unblemished quality was astonishing and he ended up buying far more than he needed.

What did supermodels eat anyway? Thinking of Melanie's healthy look, he'd guess that she ate less, but very high quality. She had none of the gauntness so common in her profession, so he worried less about calories and more about being nutrient dense and flavorful.

He'd begin with a minestrone soup. He wandered Pike Place Market, selecting the root vegetables he'd need, spring spinach for iron, and fresh herbs. It was crowded with jostling shoppers browsing the stalls. He bought a fresh-orange gelato that tasted of California sunshine.

And the flowers were everywhere in the Market. Spring in Seattle meant buckets of flowers. The strange weather this year had crossed late tulips and irises with early dahlias. He'd gone certifiably nuts, buying more flowers than food and then had to cart them all down the ten blocks to the condo.

He didn't know if Melanie was planning to be back for dinner or not, but he'd felt like cooking anyway. And he wanted to bring the Seattle spring indoors.

If he stuck around Seattle at all, he'd see if he could find some herb plants so that he could have them right in the kitchen for clipping. The mid-afternoon light shining in the condo's south and west windows would make a windowsill garden easy to cultivate.

He built the soup and started it simmering as quickly as he could. Then he unloaded his car, stacking his meager collection of boxes along the wall. The new finish on the old wood floor shone in the spattered sunlight just begging for a few nice accent rugs and new furniture, especially a decent writing chair.

He resisted the urge to unpack his boxes into the large bookcases Angelo had placed near the kitchen, obviously for a cookbook collection now probably in his high-rise home with Jo.

For the moment, he pulled the laptop out on the dining room table, but made no new progress on the novel. His attempts to distract himself with his e-mail totally failed after deleting the few messages "congratulating" him on making the leap into the unknown. An inbox he'd never caught up with in the last decade was empty in minutes. Not a single message from Constance. He slapped the cover closed before he could ask why he was expecting one. Five years of marriage and all he'd proven was that he was even stupider about women than writing novels.

He went to check on the soup, but it didn't need anything other than more time.

He'd noticed the way Melanie had left much of the bread from her *panino* behind at lunch. She hadn't made a show of it, but it was there. So carbs were an issue, but you couldn't have minestrone without good bread. Rather than a big loaf, he'd purchased small ciabatta rolls. Also, he left out the handful of pasta that he'd normally have tossed in for Constance. Constance's mom had always done it for her little girl and it was the key ingredient of minestrone, according to his wife.

His *ex*-wife.

He had to brace himself against the counter and let his head hang while trying to remember how to breathe past the pain. It was no longer a constant companion, but it did slap him when he least expected it.

"It smells wonderful in here."

Josh almost strangled himself as a gasp for breath—far too close to a sob for his taste—jerked him upright to see Melanie relocking the door behind her. He couldn't speak as the vision floated toward him. Again, that soft, unconscious sway of hip and the natural smile.

"I…" *Get your shit together Josh!* "…didn't know if you'd be around for dinner, but I made plenty. I do have to warn you, it's disgustingly healthy."

"As long as it smells the way it tastes, I'm all in." She dropped her large, wood-handled, leather designer bag on a chair and came over to stare down into the pot and breathe in deeply, releasing it with a soft sigh.

This close, he could smell her despite the aromatic mine-strone. She smelled of…*if you're going to be a writer, you can find the right word…*hope. Of glorious possibility. Simply being in her presence made him feel as if the world was a better place. Standing so close that he could easily have run his hand over her long, lovely hair, the world was filled with promise.

He stepped back, "I'm such a mess."

"You are, how?"

"I didn't mean to say that aloud."

"Too late!" She leaned back against the counter, crossed her arms comfortably and looked at him with the bluest eyes on the planet. "Give."

Evade! "First let me say: this accentless New Yorker fits you better than the French."

He shouldn't have said that. She tensed up as if he was the one now wielding the Taser.

"The slightly French supermodel is strong, foreboding, unapproachable. I can see why you chose her; she is an exceptionally formidable woman positively radiating mystique. And I can see why you left behind the…other." At least he had enough sense to not throw Paramus, New Jersey in her face.

She tensed more anyway; her arms clenched so tightly he wondered if she'd hurt herself.

"But this version of you, with the trace of Manhattan in your voice and leaning back comfortably—until I was dumb enough to start on your accent to avoid answering your question—is an equally wondrous and alarmingly attractive woman."

"Alarmingly?" She didn't sound pissed. Okay, not only pissed. Melanie also sounded intrigued, though she was keeping it off her face with that perfect control of hers suddenly clamped into place.

"Way!" was the only answer he felt safe giving before returning his attention to nursing along his soup. The silence stretched but he didn't dare look up. He took a small taste of the rich broth and decided that a little salt…no, anchovy paste would bring it to life nicely.

Speaking truth to power was said to be an extremely dangerous action undertaken only by the brave or the foolhardy. Well, he'd just made a total fool of himself, for what greater power was there over man than beauty? Maybe he could work that into his book somehow. Who was he kidding? If he ever managed to write one.

"Alarmingly."

He nodded at her choosing to make it a statement, but didn't look up.

"And you think that by turning my own judgment of myself on its head is going to get you out of answering my question of how are you a mess?"

This time when he glanced up, he could see the humor showing on her face.

"I had kind of hoped."

She flashed that killer smile that was never seen in any of

her ads or photo spreads or runway shows, then told him he was a, "Sucker! Now give."

He laughed. He couldn't help himself. Something about her filled the world with a joy he'd forgotten existed.

"How am I such a mess?" he reframed the question.

"Yes."

"Because three months ago, on the day I first met you as a matter of fact, I had a wife who loved me, living together in a condo that we'd decorated just right for us, and a great career as a food writer. Within twenty-four hours I was well on my way to losing all three."

"I know the food reviewing part. I always read your articles and reviews first, just in case I didn't have time to read the rest of the magazine. You write beautifully."

"Okay, I'll try not to grow wings and float about the room on a sheer burst of ego."

She glanced at the heavy-beamed ceiling, then back down at him, her tone dead-flat serious. "Watch your head if you do."

Melanie couldn't think of the last time she'd had a conversation like this with a man, or a woman. It was easy, fun. Even if Joshua had just torn off her mask by... How had he done it? By being nicely normal and making her soup.

Men bought her sumptuous meals she didn't want, hoping it would work in their favor—it never did. Men didn't cook one of her favorite comfort soups from scratch or make a show of ducking their heads just in case they did sprout wings. No one understood her humor. But someone just had. How curious.

So, he'd had a wife and a condo.

"What happened?"

"After five years together, Constance," the poor man winced at merely saying her name aloud, "discovered she was more interested in members of her own sex. It was amicable, and yet I still—" He turned away, not even pretending to fuss at the stove. He braced both hands on the sink and bowed his head, much as he'd been standing when she entered.

Melanie was unsure what to do, but she knew she couldn't stand to witness such pain and do nothing. She moved up beside him and began rubbing her palm up and down his back. There was no fat on his frame. He wasn't "built" like Russell or muscular from weightlifting like Angelo. He was long, lean, handsome, and hurting.

"I'm okay. Sorry," he forced himself upright. "I'm fine."

"*Oui*," she went back to her French accent hoping to elicit a small smile, but it didn't work. "You look as fine as Caesar the day his best friend stabbed him."

"No!" he faced her. "It's not like that! She—"

"Shhh…" she brushed a hand down his smooth cheek. He was trying so hard to be fair and brave no matter how it tore him up inside.

"Shhh," she stopped his next protest with her fingertips on his lips.

Quite how she came to be kissing him she would never be sure, no matter how often she thought about it. It was definitely her action to replace her fingertips with her lips, not his. And it hadn't really lasted all that long. Not really. Just long enough for Joshua to return the kiss. Just long enough for her to moan briefly as their bodies slid together like a custom fit.

She took a half step back.

Joshua didn't move to follow.

But when she went to step back farther, he reached out to stop her; just resting his fingertips on her arm, but it was enough.

"Just give me a moment."

She nodded, unable to speak.

Joshua swallowed hard, then blinked. "First, let me say thank you."

"And second?" There was a softness there she didn't often allow into her own voice, but she really wanted to know what was second.

"Well, we can never do that again."

"What?" That was about the last reaction she'd expected. What was it with the world that everyone was suddenly rejecting her? Why were—

"Wait! Stop!"

"Stop what?" She looked down at herself. She hadn't moved an inch. They still stood close enough for her to feel the heat from his body, his fingers resting so lightly on her forearm still kept her in place as if glued. Close enough to see the obvious reaction his body was having to hers. "I haven't moved."

"No, but your brain just went somewhere nasty. Here," Joshua turned down the burner under the soup and tossed a cover on the pot with an overloud clatter that made them both wince. Then he took her hand and, leading her over to the dining table, guided her into one of the chairs. Not releasing her hand, he sat in the next one after turning it to face hers.

She liked the way his hands felt. Clean, muscular. Not callused, but someone used to using his hands. He didn't crush his grip down on hers. It was the lightness of his touch that held her in place far more surely than his grasp.

"Okay," his voice was deep, husky, one she could easily melt into under different circumstances. "First—"

"You do like your lists, don't you?"

"I do. First, a kiss like that could kill a man. Way more dangerous than a Taser. You know that, right?"

She could only shake her head. He wasn't what she expected from even one sentence to the next.

"Well, it can. Damn, Melanie, that was amazing. But second,

there is no way you want to waste that kind of amazing on me no matter how much I enjoyed it."

"Why not?" The man wove words around her in circles more neatly than Donatella wrapped the latest Versace fashion.

"Remember the part where I'm a mess?"

"And I'm not?"

That rocked him back in his chair. He let go of her hand, more let it slip from his grasp than actually let go. She missed the contact.

He rubbed at his eyes for a moment. "Sorry. Wow. Told you I was a mess. You hit me with a kiss like that and you expect me to remember that you aren't some fashion goddess for whom everything is perfect."

Perfect. She was so many kinds of not perfect. She was sick of men thinking that because she was "oh so stunning" and had a successful career, that somehow made everything automatically okay.

Then he slid down a little in his chair, crossing his feet under the table—rather than outside her chair as if to cage her in—and catching his thumbs in his jeans pockets with just that exact amount of casual that men made look so easy and natural. He might be a mess, but he was a damned handsome one. He assessed her with those dark eyes. She'd worked with too many intense designers and photographers to fidget, but it was the first time in a long time she'd wanted to.

"You're in Seattle. In a borrowed condo. What is the world's best supermodel doing hiding out in Seattle?"

"I'm not hiding. And I'm not the best."

"Don't be ridiculous," he dismissed her second statement so lightly. "Yet still, you're here."

"Okay," she had to admit, "maybe it looks like I'm hiding, but I'm not." Then why was she sounding so defensive? "I'm helping Perrin."

She could see that he wasn't buying it. She could prove it,

even if it wasn't technically true. Reaching into her handbag, Melanie pulled out her new-purchased journal and dropped it into his lap, forcing him to stop looking so damn comfortable with himself in order to keep it from falling to the floor.

She went to the bath off her bedroom to let him look through her ideas. The first step away, she regretted exposing herself to him that way, but couldn't very well take it back. She had to get some space, and rinse the city off her skin with cool water. Instead, she stood staring at herself in the mirror and tried to see how he saw what he did. Melanie looked at her reflection, and only saw herself.

That was the problem.

Joshua saw the same woman she did.

JOSH FLIPPED through the two dozen pages covered in Melanie's sloppy cursive and some sketched charts that he'd have to ask her about, though two of them might have been a workload analysis. Then he went back to the first page and began reading.

Analysis of Perrin's Glorious Garb business structure and present standing in cash and orders. It was bigger than he thought, though some of the numbers were really wonky. He noticed that Melanie had returned from her bedroom and stood in her doorway looking at him still seated at the dining table studying her work.

"Did she really only have a manager and a shop clerk and herself until yesterday?"

"Day before, I helped her interview and hire two seam-stresses."

"I don't know fashion, but she looks really understaffed."

"She was. Still is," Melanie admitted.

He continued reading. Growth curves, analyses... "What's a

mob show? Is that like a runway event for the mafia or something?"

"A runway show can cost hundreds of thousands of dollars to stage. She doesn't have the cash for that and won't anytime soon. A mob show is hiring and dressing the models, but turning it into an informal show at the entrance of a major runway show. It gets attention, perhaps decent press if it's good —and it goes without saying that hers would be good. It can be almost as effective at a tenth the cost."

He looked at the timeline sketched out, "but not for six months?"

"You have to build a capacity so that you can address success when it occurs. To have a hit show and then not be able to deliver subsequent orders to customers..."

She trailed off at his nod.

"What?" She looked surprised that he understood.

"I was just thinking of some restaurants I reviewed. The chefs were masterful. And in the early days, I'd review them. Then they collapsed beneath their own inability to perform and maintain standards after the notoriety packed their establishment. It was pretty sad actually." He tried shifting in his seat, but couldn't find a comfortable position. Those first failures had been so horrid.

"I took more care later in my career, starting reading their financials and inspecting their kitchens before I'd write them up. I used to hurt for some of these poor guys, they finally land a visit by the Senior Editor of *Gourmet Week*, me, and cook their hearts out. What does he do? He sits them down and tries to explain why he won't write a review until they get their shit together. Not a pretty sight. I may have made Angelo cry back in the beginning."

Melanie moved into the room, slowly coming from the doorway back to the table. The sway of her hips, the smooth slide of long hair onto her shoulder, the way she looked at him...

And then all she did was sit back in the chair she'd occupied only minutes before. Something had changed, but he'd be damned if he knew what. He dug around in his head for what he'd just been talking about.

Soup?

No. He needed to check on it, but that wasn't it.

How they were both a mess?

She hadn't answered that, which was a lady's prerogative.

Perrin's Glorious Garb. Right. He tapped the pages filled with Melanie's writing.

"I can see this working, but do you think she can pull it off?"

Melanie didn't play coy or pretend; she simply shook her head.

He liked that clarity and honesty. He flipped through the pages once more, "There's got to be a way. This is solid. You did a really stellar job here."

He failed to notice the casual brush of fingertips that Melanie used to wipe away the tear sliding along her cheek.

"So, what are you writing?" Melanie had to talk about something to stop herself from getting a second bowl of the minestrone. It was beyond delicious.

"Crap. That's what I'm writing, drivel and crap. I didn't really expect anything else at the outset, so I'm not really upset." Joshua mopped up the remains of his second bowl with his roll. "I wish it wasn't quite such forced, amateurship, totally lame crap though."

"Tell me about it." Somewhere along the way the Ice Queen hadn't quite shattered, but she'd certainly been star-cracked. Actually, she knew the exact moment. It was when Joshua had read her notes and said they were "solid." She knew he was one of the most respected writers and business analysts in his field. She'd learned a lot about how to manage her own career from reading the business column he put in each issue of *Gourmet Week*: "Basting the Business."

Why did one outside validation from such a near total stranger mean so much more than the evidence of her banking and investment accounts? She didn't know why, but it did.

"I always thought a foodie mystery would be fun. Murder and food. There are so many great weapons: knives, poisons, gases, walk-in freezers... It just seemed like a fun idea. I've been thinking about it for years." He took up his third ciabatta roll and, finding nothing more to mop up, simply began eating it.

"But..." Breaking down, she took the last piece of her first roll to wipe her own bowl.

"But," Joshua shrugged. "I never thought about what plot I would write, who I would kill and who might be the murderer. So, I'm starting out pretty cold. An article I can fake."

"Because you've written four or five columns a week for the last decade," she cut him off.

"Okay, granted. I've had some practice so I know how to do that. Can't fake a novel. That's real writing."

"What if it wasn't?"

"Huh?"

She rested her chin on her fist, elbow on the table. It placed her a bit closer to him than she'd anticipated, but neither did she want to draw away.

"Well," she began, "I've watched designers become completely snarled when trying to create a 'showstopper'—a truly breakthrough dress. Perrin does it right. She surrounds herself with dozens of sketches and specific fabrics. I think that's part of the reason she has so much success. She keeps the results unimportant until it's done. She just plays."

"Unimportant?"

Melanie so enjoyed watching him thinking. Every expression was right on the surface.

"You mean just start writing and let it go where it goes?"

"*Absolument!* If the words aren't so precious, if the stakes were lower, wouldn't it be easier to write?"

He narrowed his eyes at her, "How are you so smart?"

She could only sit back and blink at him.

"No, don't stop now. You're on a roll."

Melanie went and dished up one more ladle of the soup, more to buy herself a little space for the new emotions running through her. He had cooked her dinner, but there was no *quid pro quo* that she could sense, he'd been generous and she'd accepted. She checked her internal tally sheet and still found no entry on it except gratitude. Joshua was gaining a presence in her thoughts in just an evening's time. *That* aspect was disconcerting.

Returning to the table, she casually nudged her chair a few inches farther away. She needed the extra distance from this man if she had any hope of keeping her shields intact.

The extra few inches didn't feel nearly far enough.

"No! No! No!" Melanie waved her licked-clean soup spoon at him.

Josh made a show of retreating to the kitchen, then began cutting up a pear and some cheese for the light dessert he'd planned.

"You start with a bang. Here, I will show you." She dug into her big purse and unearthed five novels.

"What else is in there?"

"Shut up and listen." And she began reading. It wasn't some sotto voice recitation. She read the first half dozen paragraphs of each book, giving a voice and drama to the writing. By the second one she was on her feet, by the third, she began acting out the speeches. By the fourth he'd forgotten about dessert and at the last one he was mesmerized.

Each book opened with a punch. Some character in trouble. The trouble varied. The military romantic suspense had conflict with a new commander, the mysteries with a dead body, the thriller with a car chase, and the humor book with a hilarious situation that Melanie refused to read past the first few lines.

"*Non!* What is *de la plus grande importance* isn't what they are saying. It is the punch with which they open. The first scene, the first dress in the runway show—POW!" She actually came up to him and slapped her palm against his forehead. "That is what makes the audience excited about the show, that first kick declares, 'just you wait.' The one at the end of the show is the showstopper, but the beginning, that is the powerful one."

Josh still didn't have the least inkling of where to start his book. But watching Melanie stride back and forth in her excitement, he definitely understood that a powerful woman had to be at the heart of the story. Because, *Damn!,* he had the perfect model for that character right in front of him.

CHAPTER 5

*J*osh woke at his usual five a.m. Apparently being on the West Coast simply wasn't working its way into his biorhythms. He showered, and slipped out of the condo. He exchanged a wave with the now-familiar shelter cook going in the back door just as Josh passed. The bit of routine helped ground him in the quiet city; it made him feel a little more as if he belonged.

Which was a welcome change, because nothing about last night fit into any sort of a coherent reality. Normal guys didn't spend a long quiet evening chatting with a supermodel. For the life of him, he couldn't recall what they'd talked about.

Maybe his nervous system was still in overwhelm.

He'd headed up the ten blocks of the First Avenue grade and tried to get his brain working again. Every time he did, he simply thought of Melanie.

That was it. Just Melanie.

The words had been fun. She was intelligent, well-read, and had a dry sense of humor that he tripped over every time.

Her laugh. He loved her laugh.

It had lit the condo, made it warm, filled it with life.

They'd—he could do this if he focused—talked about favorite books through a dessert of tea and crisp slices of New Zealand pears. Okay, he'd recovered that much. Oh, and powerful characters. Didn't the woman use a mirror and see herself clearly? She held herself under such tight and careful control with apparently no idea of how truly formidable she was.

He watched the ferry once again leaving the Seattle water-front under the brightening sky. Right! Travel. They'd gone on to talk favorite destinations: he and Constance had vacationed in several spots that had been promoted in the backgrounds of Melanie's photo shoots. Melanie had eaten in any number of the restaurants that he'd reviewed. They were forming a nice little mutual admiration society. J&M Mutual Admiration Society. She'd suggested they needed a logo and t-shirts.

Melanie had tried to insist on cleaning the dishes, but he hadn't thought to buy rubber gloves and he wasn't letting her risk her hands.

"I'm not frail," she'd protested.

"But I know that my fingers are not worth a gazillion dollars an hour. Go on, tell me what your hands are insured for by Lloyd's of London."

He'd meant it as a joke, but when she quoted a number in the mid-seven figures he'd responded, "I am so throwing you off the clean-up detail."

And her bright laugh had wrapped around him in thanks.

Like Odysseus, he followed the siren call of coffee through the warm spring darkness still hovering over the silence about Pike Place Market. Mama Maria would assuredly have coffee and a *cornetto* ready and waiting.

Melanie had reacted strangely to him, which shouldn't surprise him, as she was running his own emotions through the blender—on the Utterly Destroy setting. She'd smile at him and his pulse would rocket upward. She'd look grateful for being let

off the hook of washing dishes barehanded and he'd felt...
strong? Chivalrous? Something.

Once he'd thought about it, it made perfect sense how
smart she was. Even if it was unexpected at first. Careers like
hers didn't happen by accident. No matter how delectable the
food was, the restaurant failed if not properly run. When he
learned that she was her own manager and agent and negotiated her own contracts, he knew he was in the presence of
greatness.

He arrived at the back door of Angelo's faster than expected.
Again it was open to the soft morning. Maria, in a pale blue
dress and floral apron worked once again beneath the lone light
in the darkness.

"What are you making today, Maria? It smells heavenly." He
reached for a *cornetto* but she slapped his knuckles with a long
wooden spoon so fast that he never saw it coming. He sucked
on his knuckles; they really stung.

"What?" she turned to face him. "Is that the proper way to be
greeting a woman? I expect at least a hug and a kiss upon the
cheek before you steal any of my breakfasts."

"Right. Sorry." He came around the counter and bent down
to give her a hug and a European-style peck upon each cheek.
He kissed her on the forehead for good measure. It was only
after he did so that he felt the heat rising to his cheeks. He'd
never hugged Maria before, felt he barely knew her.

"Good, boy." Maria waved him toward the coffee pot. "You
are family now, you can get your own coffee." She returned to
rolling out the dough, then looked up at him as he stood rooted
to the ground. Maria smiled and patted his cheek with a floured
hand.

He shuffled off to get his coffee. By the time he returned to
the stool he'd occupied yesterday, a pair of *cornetti* were waiting
on a plate. Even the walk and the strong coffee weren't enough
to clear his head.

"What are you doing to me, Maria?" She'd cast some sort of strange spell over him and he couldn't shake it off.

"Me. I do nothing. You do it to yourself."

"If that's true, then I'm in real trouble."

Her laughter was bright and musical.

"I can't believe some cad married you before I came along."

"Ah," her smile turned radiant. "Hogan Stanford is the perfect man for me. Fear not, you will find the perfect woman for you."

"I did," his own bitterness mixed with the next sip of coffee and he set it down with an overloud clatter in the quiet kitchen, only barely managing to not spill it again.

"No. You may think you did, but she proved you wrong. It is clear just from looking at you that she is the one who left, more the foolish woman. The right woman does not do such a thing. Men are often foolish, but a smart woman would know what she had and keep it close."

He was tired of telling the story, of defending Constance. Even as he had the thought, he recalled Melanie's fingertips on his lips. And then her kiss. It was totally inappropriate. He didn't want a rebound relationship, especially not with Melanie because she deserved so much more than assuaging his need to be with someone again—no matter how briefly.

But—and he tried his best to ignore the feeling of disloyalty to Constance—Melanie's kiss was far more powerful than her beauty. One of them had moaned with how glorious it felt, and he still wasn't sure whether or not it was him. The sheer power of his desire to devour the woman on the spot had been so startling that it was enough to break the spell of that brief kiss, at least for that sufficient instant to allow him to step back.

"Well," Maria was staring at him with her hands resting on her hips, "that was clearly a very pleasant thought." Her smile said that she knew much more than she was saying. He didn't want to hear it.

"Perhaps I should go write."

Maria returned to her preparations for the day, "If you can."

Unwilling to face that question either, he retreated to the darkened restaurant and the table that Angelo had said was his. He sat down and began setting up.

Maria followed moments later with the coffee and untouched *cornetti* that he'd forgotten to take with him. She gave him a hug from the side and kissed him on top of the head.

"Such a good boy."

He watched her walking back to the kitchen. What did she know that he didn't?

"PERRIN, I need to see those e-mails," Melanie had done it. It had only taken ten minutes walking around the Belltown neighborhood before entering Perrin's Glorious Garb, but she'd found the nerve somewhere.

Perrin flapped a hand toward a stack of paper at the corner of the cutting table. "I printed them all." She had finished clearing the far end of the table and fluffed out a couple yards of royal blue. A tall pile of jewel tones stood as a protective barricade between them down the middle of the table.

Karissa and Clem glanced at her with interest, but then each noticed that the other had stopped working, so they both returned to the woman's business suit they were copying in two different sizes—a little competition was a useful thing. The suit hanging on the rack between them was a powder blue, with a thin black pinstripe that just reeked of femininity and power. The overall cut and lapels were so retro that they could well be the next "new."

Melanie turned from the enticement of closer inspection, or perhaps trying it on. She could see on the rack just how masterful she'd look in it. With a dark-charcoal blouse for daytime and the jacket open, without the blouse and the jacket buttoned in the evening—the closures high enough that even a strongly figured woman could wear it.

Most clothes like this could only be worn by the most flat-chested. Perrin designed for women who had shape as well. Perhaps the influence of her friendship with Cassidy and especially Jo.

Once she had the thought, Melanie knew that was the answer. They three women were so close that they were integrated right into each other's subconscious. And she did *not* like the stab of envy that speared into her heart. To have such friends was beyond a gift, it was a miracle—one that had passed her completely by. She barely knew Perrin, yet she was fast becoming the best friend Melanie had ever had. *Impossible! Oui,* impossibly sad but it was all she had.

By the time Melanie had finished her inspection, Perrin was whacking at the royal blue with a rotary cutter. Smooth efficient slices with no pattern. Were the designs so clear in her head that she could cut them freehand, or was that only for mockup? Melanie was a little too daunted to ask, just in case Perrin really was that skilled.

Perrin was so studiously ignoring her, that Melanie knew every move she made was being closely observed.

Melanie turned to the stack of e-mails and began to read. There were many more e-mails than there had been letters, but the quality was mostly lower. She rapidly sorted aside the stupid "offers" from agents and managers who wanted to control Perrin for however much they could bleed out of her. Two she didn't simply set aside, she tore them to shreds and threw them in the garbage. She knew those scam artists and didn't want their name in Perrin's shop—what they'd done to some models they'd managed to latch onto had been horrible, career-ruining horrible.

"These two names, and I will give you a list of three more,

you must delete their e-mail as soon as it arrives. They are pollutants, not people."

"What names?"

Melanie rattled them off, added another for good measure. "I will write them for you so that you do not forget."

"No need, I've got it. Thanks, I was worried about that kind of thing."

Melanie never needed to write down such things either. Her respect for Perrin's mind went up another small notch. How much had she made the same mistake about Perrin that others made about her? They saw the flighty artist and missed the sharp businesswoman so easily.

Well, she would take a lesson from Joshua and no longer underestimate Perrin. It would be difficult, Perrin's chosen self-protective persona was as polished as her own.

Back to the e-mails. The wannabe designers were all so overeager. Some of the more professional ones had included images from their collections. On one set of images, which didn't have an attached e-mail, Perrin had made some notes down the side. The designs were interesting, but the eye was young. Perrin designed for women, but this designer sketched for teens. And did it well.

"Perrin, whose are these? If you ever want to do a youth line, you might consider hiring this designer. It would be an exceptionally fine place for beginning."

Until that moment, Perrin had been assiduously focused on cutting and pinning more of the royal blue. As soon as Melanie held up the sketches, Perrin stopped and her entire manner shifted. Her smile was huge, "Those are Tammy's."

Melanie looked at them again in awe, "I thought she was thirteen."

"Fourteen next month."

"*Merde!*"

"I stuck them in hoping you'd like them. I can't judge because I love her too much. I never imagined a stepdaughter. Actually she's my daughter since I adopted her the same day Bill married me, but that freaks me out too much to really think about. She's young enough that I could have had her if I'd had her while still in high school. But a stepdaughter, okay, daughter who is so skilled at design already just makes me all..." Perrin did a shimmy that might have been a lot like a firecracker about to explode.

"They are: well done, creative, age-appropriate," she ticked off on her fingers, trying not to feel as if she was channeling Joshua's passion for numbered lists. "You seriously need to consider these designs as the basis for a product line. A separate product line."

"Her own line?" Perrin tasted the idea and stared at the ceiling as she toyed with the idea.

Melanie realized just how little prepared Perrin was for what was about to happen to her, no matter how smart. That should have been an automatic next-step thought, instead it had to be given to her to think about.

Melanie went back to her sorting. Several of the e-mails were overlaps with the letters. She checked the dates; frustrated by no response to their electronic messages, they had gone to paper-based pleas. But for the most part, there were at least as many new opportunities here as in the folder. If only twenty percent of these came through, Perrin's business wasn't going to grow, it was going to skyrocket upward. Whereas her own was...

Melanie clambered off the stool and to her feet. She looked for somewhere else to sit, but realized she didn't want to sit. She didn't want to sew. She saw Perrin—still glowing from the compliment to her new daughter—leaning in to explain a particularly tricky pattern piece to Karissa and Clem.

The soft-rap tune on the radio was getting on her nerves;

something about a geek in pink. The next one would be about models no one wanted to see any longer.

Out front would be no better. From here she could see customers in the front of the shop. There was so much purpose here, everyone had something to do and she...was useless.

Melanie had never been useless. More importantly, she would never again depend upon another person for her state of mind. She closed the folders, picked up her bag, and wished Perrin *À bientôt.* No one on the outside looking at her must ever know what was wrong.

Yet Perrin clearly sensed something by her surprised expression, but Melanie made it out the door before it registered fully enough for Perrin to do more than look at her oddly. A clean getaway.

That's what she had to do. She had to get away. She didn't belong here. She belonged in... She didn't even know where the swimsuit shoot was this year. That was insider-only knowledge, and for eight straight years she'd been in the know.

Well, the magazines weren't going to control her mind either. Her mother had done her best to twist and control Melanie's mind, as well as Melanie's body to her own ends. That too was done. So, perfectly in control—calm, collected, and throwing a walk that made men stop and stare—she strode past the shops of Belltown and then headed south.

It was late morning. Hole-in-the-wall restaurants were blocking as much of the sidewalk as they dared with small steel tables and artfully rusting chairs throwing off her purposeful stride. Little boutiques were displaying wares not half the quality of Perrin's. These were shops she might have normally browsed, but it would be a pointless waste.

When she reached Pike Place Market it meant she was a third of the way back to the condo. She would pack, find a flight, and go home. Hopefully, she would get there before the wave of depression crushed down on her and left her unpresentable to friends and fodder for her worst enemies, the paparazzi. With a single unguarded moment, they could capture and damage a career, even one like hers. And news of the swimsuit issue loss would be out by now. Add that into...

She stopped. She couldn't breathe. Bending over to rest her hands on her knees, her hair almost brushing the dirty cobbles, didn't help. All she could see was the cobblestones. No air. She leaned against a handy wall until her head stopped spinning enough for her to think. To recognize where she was so that she could continue on her way. She was in front of...

Angelo's?

She'd been headed to the condo; straight down First Avenue. How had she ended up in the heart of Pike Place Market? Granted it was only a block aside from her escape route...

Oh. Some part of her that was still functioning knew she should say *merci* to Maria and *au revoir* to Joshua. He hadn't been at the condo when she woke, so maybe he was here writing.

JOSH LOOKED up from the pit of despair into the warm sunshine of hope. The transition was a shock to both his brain and his libido. If yesterday his writing had been crap, this morning he had crawled into the outhouse, then ducked down the hole for a lengthy soak.

He took a moment to appreciate the wonder that was Melanie. Her casual wear could shame, well, any supermodel that wasn't her and all mere mortals. Rumpled leather cavalier boots to mid-calf, skinny jeans that showed the advantage of perfect legs even when hidden away, a sunshine yellow blouse whose loose form didn't reveal, but a sharp leather vest that suggested very strongly. And those eyes. Cornflower blue offset against her light golden hair.

"I'm leaving."

"Thank god."

She looked at him quizzically.

"I think Mama Maria put a special hex on me. If yesterday was crap, today is completely unmentionable in decent company." He slapped his laptop in his bag and rose to his feet.

It was only when he was standing eye to eye with her that he saw the stiffly square set of her shoulders, the grim determination in her look. He knew that look. Head down and striding straight into a headwind come hell or damnation. It was the only way he'd survived the last three months.

Her words finally registered. She was leaving? Like leaving Seattle? *Nope. Not no way. Not no how.* He didn't know why the voice in his head was so vehement on that point, but it was.

"Uh huh. Leaving? Good. Let's go." Purposely misunderstanding her. He offered his arm, and when she hesitated, he took her hand and tucked it into his elbow simply because he wanted to. She left it there as he guided her out of the restaurant. He liked the sense of connection.

She seemed almost nerveless, even ethereal as he led her down the rough brick of Post Alley. The late morning crowd of tourists swirled about them. The piano guy had his little roll-around upright piano on a street corner and was knocking out a very creditable version of Joplin's *The Entertainer.* Josh tossed his spare change in the busker's bucket; he didn't want to risk dislodging Melanie's hand to reach for his wallet.

In silence he led her deeper into the Market. He'd expected her to unravel at least a little bit as they moseyed past the overflowing flower stands, but their lush scents and brilliant sprays of color didn't touch her.

So, keeping them in pace with the slow-moving crowd—but not stopping to admire the sights—they were soon clear of the flower, produce, and artisanal sausage merchants. They bypassed the pasta stall with over thirty flavors of pasta from chocolate to strawberry to—he had to glance over his shoulder to be sure of the last—licorice. He made a note to try that someday, perhaps paired with honeyed peaches for a dessert—the black pasta and golden fruit making an interesting contrast. Down the stairs by the tea merchant, they passed the parrot store and a bagel shop.

It only took a few minutes before he had led her under the viaduct highway, across Alaskan Way, and out onto the vacant Pier 62. All of the other piers along Seattle's deep waterfront were filled with tourist or commerce activities: restaurants, giant Ferris wheel, ferry terminal, the Seattle Aquarium. For some reason, this pier and the adjoining one created a couple of acres of unoccupied rough wood planking. A few people wandered the open expanse, but it was actually a very private place right at the heart of the Northwest's largest city.

He led her out to the far corner of the pier. Behind them the city soared and bustled. Ahead of them the dark blue waters of Elliot Bay were dotted with green-trimmed white ferries, container ships headed for the big orange port cranes to the left, a couple of sailboats skimming along under the light breeze. A massive cruise ship was just pulling away from the next pier to the north. The city proper was bordered to the south and north by house-dappled hills, straight ahead the snow-capped peaks of the Olympic Mountains were so bright in the sun that it was hard to look at them.

Melanie remained beside him, unmoving, unspeaking.

Josh bided his time, letting the soothing breeze—pleasantly cool off the water on a calm day—wash over them. When he turned at last to face her, because he couldn't stand not seeing her a moment longer, she looked a little calmer.

"Okay, Ms. Secretly-I'm-a-mess-no-matter-how-incredibly-I-present-myself-to-the-world. What happened?"

In answer, Melanie simply turned into his arms and lay her head on his shoulder. She clung to him as if he were the Rock of

Gibraltar rather than a lost soul himself. Well, if she needed him to be strong, he would be.

His arms naturally slid around her and he came to appreciate so many things at once. Slender yet strong, hair even softer than it looked, just meant to be stroked gently, and he was right the first time—she absolutely smelled of hope, hope and summertime.

MELANIE COULD FEEL the day brightening, one tiny bit at a time. She knew she was being irrational, knew her past wasn't really a vicious bounty hunter seeking to repossess her soul; it only felt that way. Except it didn't feel that way with Joshua.

From the moment she'd taken his arm, it was as if all her willpower was gone. Her panic-level desperation to run, to get somewhere safe, had simply drained away. When she was losing control, he had simply taken it. Then he'd brilliantly led her here where the people didn't press about her so.

She had meant to give him a brief hug of thanks, but her body had other ideas and she'd clung to him like a lover, never wanting to move again. His arms were strong, solid. His shoulder perfect to lean her cheek on. Right at the base of his neck was a place she could go to hide for a long, long time. Not even to hide. She could almost...what? Be content here?

His skin was warm against her nose and forehead. His soft dark hair, which needed a trim soon, tickled her temple. Her nose couldn't place him except to say, "male." Joshua exuded "strong male" as if it were a new designer fragrance. So, instead of a brief hug or a tentative embrace, she simply allowed herself to appreciate the soft stroke of his hands down her back. To enjoy the moment.

Before she was ready, his chest rumbled with the repeated voicing of his question. How was she supposed to know what happened? She'd simply needed get away before the world collapsed on her head.

Her desire to leave her momentary haven was non-existent, but Joshua kissed her atop her head and then pushed her back a half pace to study her, keeping his hands on her waist. She wanted to imagine that her shields were up, but knowing that he always saw straight through them, she stopped trying.

"Well, whatever it was..." he continued as he studied her.

She could still feel the deep rumble of his voice where she'd left a hand resting on his chest.

"I'm guessing that you've given yourself a pretty thorough scare. I find it hard to imagine you being scared of anything, but that's my guess."

"Will you cut that out!"

His grin told her that he knew exactly what she meant and the answer was: no, he wouldn't. "Bugs you, huh?"

"No one sees past my shields."

"Superman and me, we're tight. Drinking buddies, you know."

She didn't know whether to smile or poke him sharply in the solar plexus, so she did both eliciting a satisfying whoosh though she hadn't hit him hard enough to do more.

He took his hands from her waist to rub at his chest and looked at her in surprise.

"You better just keep your x-ray vision to yourself. You start looking through my vest and I really will Taser you but good."

"Yes, ma'am. I can't speak for my imagination, but I can promise on my x-ray vision. It's regrettably limited in such cases."

"What is it with men and their imagination? Women spend notably little time mentally undressing men."

"Damn and I had such hopes."

Melanie, having said that and having returned her hand to the center of his chest in apology for striking him, now found that she could imagine Joshua unclothed. As a matter of fact, it was disconcertingly easy to do so.

"Distract me," the request sort of blurted out of her.

Joshua looked her right in eyes for a long moment, appeared to be on verge of suggesting a sure-fire distraction that would earn him a truly sharp punch in the solar plexus; a Taser was not the only element of her self-defense training. But rather than speaking his thought, his eyes slid aside and studied the world around them. Something across the water had him narrowing his eyes for a moment.

"How's your blood sugar?"

Not, "are you hungry?" It was a more personal question of whether her current chaos of emotions was due to low blood sugar. In the body condition she maintained, blood sugar was at times a delicate balance. She tested her own feelings. Nope, that had been genuine panic.

"I'm fine for the moment," she told him.

"Excellent, c'mon," he brightened like a little boy. "Got a treat for you if you have the afternoon free and don't mind spending it with me." Once again Joshua offered his arm. This time she was glad to take it, enjoyed the connection through the light cloth of his button-down shirt, just open enough at the throat to hint at the strength she'd felt there.

He led her south along the waterfront until they reached the big ferry terminal. She was always amazed at how many of the big white and forest-green ferries there were, shuttling back and forth from the Seattle waterfront. Of course with the island-cluttered Puget Sound nearly chopping the state in half from north to south, it made sense.

"I reviewed this great little place over on Bainbridge Island a couple of years back. Perfect for lunch."

When the boat arrived, he guided her not to the bow of the boat pointing out to the Sound, but to the stern of the passenger deck several stories above where the cars loaded. Most people passed into the main cabin through the big doors heavy enough to keep even the nastiest storms at bay. She and Joshua stood in the late morning sunlight at the rearmost point and watched the loading process. A small fleet of bicycles and motorcycles zoomed aboard, then a long stream of cars, shuttled off to the correct spots for the crossing by orange-clad ferry workers.

A glance up revealed the city, close and looming above them. The massive double-tiered roadway of the Alaskan Way Viaduct, so crowded with cars and trucks, as if they were trying to use it as much as possible before it was replaced by the new tunnel being bored beneath the waterfront. Skyscrapers capped it off, made far taller than they actually were by the steep hill climbing up through the city.

"They all look so intent, don't they?" Joshua's words drew her attention back to the loading. "Even the ones too out of their element to follow the ferry loader's instructions; all in such a hurry to arrive."

Without Joshua's words, it would have been no more than a stream of cars, but it was more. She began to see and appreciate the scene, but her interest paled soon enough. There was a sameness to all of that focused intent and she found it exhausting to witness.

"Let's go explore." The ferry was huge, holding a couple hundred cars in the lower two decks and at least two thousand passengers in the two upper decks.

"They're almost done," he assured her. "There's something I want you to see."

So she waited, rubbing shoulders with Joshua and waiting for the world to finish and get on with it. After the last car, there was a lot of very coordinated activity: stringing up ropes and safety nets, hand signals with some shore-side worker, raising of ramps. A glance at Joshua, but no, that isn't what he was waiting for. He remained still, quiet, a calm center.

She did her best to emulate him.

The ferry engine's roared to life with a deep rumble that shook the steel decking.

"Here," Joshua was leaning on the fresh-painted dark-green railing staring intently down.

Melanie followed his gaze.

The ferry slowly dragged itself from beneath the over-hanging ramp, and then she spotted a narrow gap of water. With a bellowing blast of its horn, loud enough to hurt her ears and big enough to claim the ferry's right of passage out into the waters, the boat began gathering speed. The propellers kicked up a massive swirl of aerated water, temporarily disrupting the Sound's dark blue.

And then she felt it. Like a breath of fresh air. As hypnotized as the proverbial deer in the headlights, she was mesmerized by the spectacle of Seattle slipping away from them. It was a visceral rush that coursed through her body as if they were leaving the world behind. *Parfait!* Absolutely perfect!

"This must what it's like to go into space," Joshua's voice mixed with the engine's deep rumble.

It truly felt as if she was leaving the planet. There was a heady sense of liberation. Any worries or memories she'd been having were now back there on the land. And with each passing second, this great steel behemoth of a boat was taking them farther and farther away, out of trouble's easy clutches. She felt light, free.

Melanie took Joshua's face in her hands and kissed him, really kissed him. Not that intriguing brush of lips in the condo last night. This was a toe-curling kiss and his need was no less than hers. But what had started as a first burst of joy, grew deeper, gentler, but more intent. She was soon wondering just what the other men she'd kissed in her life had been up to, because this was like none of them.

Finally Joshua pulled her into a hug too close to kiss. They simply wrapped their arms around each other, leaned their cheeks together, and held on.

He whispered in her ear, "I was right. Your kiss. One hundred percent lethal."

"Guess we've died and gone to heaven."

"If it isn't, don't tell me, because I don't want to know." Then he took her hand in his before turning to look at the boat. "Now we should go explore."

CHAPTER 6

They wandered about the ferry from one end to the other. Josh led Melanie up into the wind of the mostly open upper deck where her hair streamed behind her like a great banner, dancing in the brisk wind. He pointed out the Alki lighthouse perched at Seattle's westernmost point with Mount Rainier soaring skyward as a glorious backdrop and joked that they were beyond anyone finding them now.

"Free at last. Free at last. Thank God almighty, we're free at last!" he shouted to the shining sky as Melanie sparkled the air with her laughter. She made him feel a dozen feet tall.

As if her kiss hadn't already done that.

For just this afternoon, for just this moment, he would allow himself to simply enjoy the company of a gorgeous and fascinating woman. He wouldn't be Mr. Food Writer. Nor would he permit Mr. Divorced Loser in either. Not even Mr. Wannabe-novelist who kept writing drivel.

He'd be simply Josh, who had just received a life-changing kiss that simply couldn't be real. No one gave of themselves the way Melanie had just given to him. If he didn't know he was on the rebound, he could start thinking some pretty amazing thoughts about the woman who had yet to relinquish his hand.

For their arrival at Bainbridge Island, he led her to the very bow of the boat in time to be at the forefront of the crowd. That gave them prime viewing space along the front rail as the boat cruised into Eagle Harbor and snuggled up to the ferry dock.

"I only had an hour to explore this town when I was here. Bainbridge Island, both the town and the island are actually called B. I., has a lot of money. High-end rural but within commuting range to Seattle. So there's a lot of tasty eating and shopping here."

They wandered the streets, actually the street. Most of Bainbridge was on a single street a few blocks long. They stopped at a wine store, where Josh was talked into a local loganberry wine. Then the shop owner went on to sell him a local artisanal blue cheese to go with it for a dessert.

"Wine and food shops are as dangerous to me as hardware stores to most guys. Just," he made a point of opening the shopping bag once they were out of sight of the shop and looking down in overdramatic disbelief. "Just stop me if I ever do that again."

"Deal. If you'll…" Melanie came to a halt beside him and looked in a bookstore window. "You can't let me go in there."

Melanie didn't look the least bit like a bookworm, but her near lust for the bookshop was impossible to mistake. Then he recalled that she'd hauled five novels out of her handbag last night, one still sporting the charge slip. He held the door for her and shooed her inside.

"Hey!"

"I can't be the only weak-fish on this outing. Go find a book."

She did come away with a book on Northwest weavings. But he ended up being the big spender with two new thrillers, a mystery, and four books on the history of Seattle.

"Okay, we just have to get off this street," he complained

when they were back in the sunlight. "How's the peckishness level?"

"Rising. I saw that cute diner by the ferry."

"The Streamliner. Yep, they're tasty. I have their cookbook too. I'm going to do you one better."

MELANIE STARED at the bright blue sign on a stainless-steel diner two blocks off the main drag.

"The Madison Diner, founded in 1953? This looks like the sort of *dîneur* that hasn't changed the grease in its fryers *since* 1953," she teased him, though it did smell splendid; comfort-food smells wafted through the doors so thickly she could taste them on the air.

She wore her French accent in public like a second skin. It kept people at a distance, though Joshua simply ignored such barriers and continued to treat her the same. She was having a terrible time this afternoon remaining focused on any one thing that wasn't Joshua. She turned firmly away to inspect their diner.

It did look as if it had been teleported right out of the fifties. Stainless steel as far as the eye could see with metallic blue panels. The roof and building corners were all rounded. Once inside, she wasn't the least surprised to find round steel stools along the counter with red leatherette padding. Small booths that really were perfect for shooting greaser movies.

It all looked...cozy.

For an instant, the outside world was juxtaposed. Perrin's beautiful and quirky store was also a 1950s diner motif. Take away the tables and the cook line, replace the chattering tourists with fashion-forward mannequins...

She shoved the image aside hard. She didn't want to think

about the real world. She wanted to remain here, in the present, with Joshua.

Melanie closed her eyes for a moment and breathed in deeply. It smelled heavenly. Not as heavenly as Josh, but enough to make her stomach rumble a little. The waitress, a pretty brunette, obviously recognized Melanie but made no big deal of it which was a surprising change from the standard.

Soon they were tucked in their own booth, he with a fresh-squeezed lemonade and her with iced tea.

"Let me guess," Joshua was using the little-bit-too-full-of-himself teasing tone of his, "a bowl of soup or a salad."

"*Non.* With such a menu, there are too many choices. But I see one something, so there is only one choice for me." He made many guesses, but none were even close. "You, however, would appear to be a mushroom Swiss cheeseburger guy. Extra fries."

"Nailed."

He snorted with laughter when she ordered the Blazing Buffalo Chicken Burger marinated in Buffalo chicken-wing hot sauce, with no bun but an extra side of hot sauce.

"I may have to eat French and *une très petite portion* when the reporters find me, but I think we are sufficiently far from any reporters here."

"Don't know. The *Bainbridge Island Review* could be desperate for a front-page story. They're sending some poor stringer this very moment to interview the most beautiful woman to ever mosey through their shops."

She ignored him. Well, not entirely. The booths weren't designed with two people six-feet tall in mind. Their knees kept bumping as Joshua decently tried to move his aside. She finally leaned her knee against his and left it there. Not as connected as holding hands, but far more welcome than unwelcome.

She'd never been one to hold hands. Melanie had deigned to parade on many a man's arm, though rarely with any of the benefits that the paparazzi always assumed. This was the first moment all day that she'd thought about her hands. They were one of her highest paid features and she protected them assiduously. Her first million had been made on her hands alone.

Even as she surreptitiously inspected them, she knew that she would hold hands with Joshua again if he offered the opportunity, despite the risk of an unsightly stretch or crease.

"So, are you ready yet to talk about what freaked you out this morning?"

"*Non!*" But he'd surprised her. She gently tested her emotional state. No sign of the looming depression that had her scurrying back to New York. Instead, she had been quite enjoying herself. Was still enjoying herself.

"If you don't, it's just going to lie in there and fester."

"That does not sound so enjoyable, does it?"

"*Non!*" he replied clearly to tease her again about her chosen accent.

"Crap!" She gave it full Jersey-twang which earned her the laugh she'd been hoping for. It also made her feel just kindly enough toward him to begin the story of the last week.

"THEY DROPPED you from the swimsuit issue? Damn it! I always looked forward to—" Josh tried to stop his mouth, but it was a moment too late.

Melanie lowered her fork slowly back to her plate of half-finished chicken burger. If he didn't stop the ice shield descending like a cloak from above before it covered her, Melanie would be as surely gone as if she'd run straight to the airport.

"Wow! Did that ever come out wrong or what?"

"*Oui!*" Her accent was back in full force.

"Don't I get one screw-up? You admitted to ogling my restaurant reviews."

"Mon dieu! 'Ogling' is not the operative word and you know it." She was carefully dabbing her mouth with her napkin; her eyes no longer focused on him, instead inspecting the cook line as if the fry cook who clearly sampled too much of his own wares was suddenly of greatest interest. Soon her knee would no longer be against his and he'd be a goner.

"Hey, if I can't admire your art, why is it okay for you to admire mine?"

"Because it was not my art you were admiring."

Josh saw his one thin chance of recovery and leapt for it like a man drowning.

"But it is."

The cloak's descent paused, but it had already covered her perfectly still hands.

He took a bite of his burger to appear casual, but didn't taste it. With a single phrase, he'd become just like every rutting goat out there. Which he really wasn't. The chance to see that much beauty in one place had always stunned him. There was something else...but he couldn't quite put his finger on it.

"How is it my art?"

"You have studied how to place yourself, how to present yourself in such a way that you create an emotion. Lust in some. In others, and I like to think I'm one, it creates a deep appreciation for the beautiful, the powerful, and—" The thought that had skittered aside moments before crashed back in on him and he stopped, unable to continue, unable to think. If he didn't swallow soon, he'd choke and he couldn't manage even that except by great conscious effort.

"It creates what?"

He looked up at Melanie and tried to make sense of her question, but he couldn't.

"It creates—" she must have finally noticed his shock.

Josh knew the shock was there. He could feel it. A wall that momentarily locked him safely away from the worst of his own emotional storm.

"Joshua?" Melanie had dropped her accent and reached her hand tentatively toward his arm.

He shook his head. "I never bought a single swimsuit issue. I saw them. Enjoyed them. Enjoyed you in them. But I didn't buy them." His voice sounded so neutral, so perfectly normal.

"I don't understand."

"Neither did I." His ex-wife was the one who'd always bought them, year after year.

"So," Josh leaned back on the bow railing of the ferry. They had their own little section of the foredeck to themselves. Slouching back, facing away from the view, provided him the perfect position to watch Melanie as she watched the approaching city.

She'd caught her hair back in some intricate French braid that appeared effortless to create and was exotically beautiful to look at. But from his vantage, what it did was keep her hair—as much as he liked it down—clear of her face. Her emotions were so visible against those fine features, it was incredibly intimate.

Especially after talking through his marriage and divorce in such excruciating detail. That she still looked at him at all was a wonder.

He liked this moment of intimacy, ignoring that it couldn't last once they were ashore. For once they landed, she would again be the world's most sought-after supermodel—one blip did not destroy a career like hers no matter what she thought—and he would continue to be an unholy mess who couldn't write.

"So," he started again, hoping he could recover his train of thought when faced with such breathtaking beauty. "You never did explain what upset you this morning."

"*Non,* I did not explain such a thing and now I shall not, not to such a cur."

"Why am I a cur now?"

"Because you did not buy your own issue of the magazine. If you had, instead of mooching your wife's copy, I might still have been in this year's issue. *Tant pis!*"

"Say what?"

" 'Too bad!' Loser."

"Can't win for losing."

"Precisely. And you, my tall and handsome *chien,* have lost this round."

"At least you didn't call me *chienne.*" Being called a bitch was never his first choice.

"You may be a dog, Joshua, but you are definitely a very male one."

He could spar words with her forever, she made it so much fun. Though he'd definitely need to work on his high school French if they were going to spar in two languages.

A glance over his shoulder showed the half hour crossing was about fifteen minutes gone.

"Okay. From here to the shore is a quarter hour. If you answer the question, I promise I won't ask again."

"Ever?"

"At least not for tonight. Best offer I've got."

She grimaced and turned her back on him, leaving him to admire other features of her. With her hair back in its thick braid, the line of her neck was revealed. A trim waist his hands actually ached to touch again. And her curves that embodied the epitome of elegantly feminine.

He was about to do something to let her off the hook when she spoke, it was soft enough he had to start forward to hear it over the brisk wind and the rumble of the ferry's engines.

"I was sitting with Perrin. And I knew what to do. I knew what she would need to be an enormous success rather than be closed within a year without knowing what hit her. There is no third path, no safe middle ground. Her talent will have too much impact."

"Wonderful. Take the high road," he spoke over her shoulder because she didn't turn and he didn't dare touch her.

"You don't understand, Joshua. I said that *I* knew what to do. She doesn't. She couldn't; not even if I were to explain it all. And she wouldn't want to. But I could."

Josh waited. They were so close. He knew the shore was sliding near, but he didn't look away; couldn't risk her changing the topic.

"But I don't know this woman, the one who thinks she knows what it would take to launch Perrin. I know the model. Her I invented. Her I know how to control. I don't know this other person. I don't know her any better than…"

She didn't need to finish the sentence.

He knew that the person she didn't know was the one that was sweeping him off his feet—the one that was Melanie and not the model and business superwoman. He took her gently by the shoulders and turned her to face him. There were tears starting from her eyes.

"Melanie."

She nodded uncertainly.

He kissed her.

She kissed him back, but there wasn't any heat behind it, nor did he expect any. "What was that for?"

"Because I wanted to."

She scowled at him through her silent tears. He brushed them aside with gentle strokes of his thumb.

"Melanie."

"Kiss me again and I just might get around to actually Tasering you."

"You are the most magnificent, powerful, exceptional woman I've ever met. The mere idea that you could lose yourself while you're doing something you love is laughable. It's so laughable and fallible that it takes you down from the ridiculously high pedestal you live on and makes you momentarily accessible to us mere mortals. When you're down here, I get to kiss you."

"So," Melanie blinked into the wind. "You're saying I have to keep screwing up to get a kiss."

"It's one way."

MELANIE COULD SEE the shore fast approaching, the Seattle skyline once again towering above them.

Melanie was no closer to making a decision about how to help Perrin. Working for her temporarily wouldn't be enough. Stepping in and making sure Perrin was a success would be throwing away a career that Melanie had spent two decades building, and she wasn't about to do that.

She did know one thing though.

So she threw herself at Joshua and drove him back against the thankfully stout railing hard enough for him to grunt. And then she wrapped her arms around his neck and kissed him the best she knew how.

Kissed him until the madness in her head quieted enough for her to relish the heat and the power of this man in her arms.

Kissed him until she no longer feared she'd shatter and be dispersed to the four winds. Until she felt totally present and there was only the here and now and their shared need for each other.

It was heady, breathtaking, and it left her torn between singing and laughter, both of which she only rarely did, and then did it alone—until Joshua had pulled the laughter out of her and into the open.

Her singing? She'd keep that in the shower.

CHAPTER 7

*A*s they were walking off the ferry, discussing dinner ideas, Melanie's phone buzzed with a message. It was the first call in days and she scrabbled for it. Perhaps one of the models on the swimsuit shoot had broken a nail—she'd seen beginners panic for less—or had been eaten by a shark—she could always hope.

But the text showed a local number.

Meet us at 5- the Fabulous Five

It was four thirty now. And she knew exactly who the four were and where they were meeting, the fifth puzzled her. She slowed to a halt at the top of the exit gangway where commuters were queuing up to board the ferry back to their island homes.

All of the surety she'd felt moments before evaporated. Joshua noticed, of course. They were so in tune that their bodies practically hummed in harmony. Maybe she'd let a little of her singing out of the shower. Was Josh down with Tunstall or B.o.B,? Maybe he was more of a Taylor Swift-Carrie Underwood cute blonde country-singer sort.

Gods she was losing her mind.

"Kiss me."

He only hesitated a moment. She thought something dark wandered across his thoughts, but it was gone by the time their lips met. The kiss grounded her but did little for her suddenly jittery stomach.

"*Merci.* I think that you are on your own for dinner tonight, *mon ami* Joshua."

"Good news, my friend?" he nodded down to the phone she still clutched like a baseball ready to pitch across a mound or a plate or wherever they pitched such things.

"*Je ne sais pas.*"

"No idea? Do you want me to go with you?"

"*Non.* Go write, find Russell, something like that."

She turned to go but he stopped her with strong hands until she looked at him.

"Are you sure you will be okay?" The warmth and care... She wasn't used to it. It was always just a ploy... By anyone, except for Joshua. How many more things would she think, "except for Joshua?"

"No," might as well be honest. "I'm not at all sure. But you tell me that I am invincible, *oui?*"

"Damn straight!" he sounded far more assured than she felt.

"Then I shall simply go and be *incroyable!*"

"Of course you will. You already are incredible." Then he swept her into a kiss that had her winding her arms and a leg about him and holding on to her newly discovered personal anchor.

The round of applause they received from the outbound commuters did little to boost her certainty, other than knowing she too had to go.

———

"RUSSELL, DUDE. RESCUE ME." *From myself! Josh thought loudly. I'm head over heels with a woman totally out of my league.*

"Hey, that you, Josh?" Russell answered over the phone.

Josh admitted that it was, "I really need a high-octane distraction."

"How about a high proof one?" Russell gave him directions to his place. He'd never been to Russell and Cassidy's condo just a few blocks north of the Market in Belltown, but it was easy enough to find.

When he arrived, Russell let him in and pointed toward the kitchen. "Grab a beer or something. We're out on the deck."

Josh dropped his and Melanie's shopping bags by the door, one of hers was bright pink and clearly from a dress shop.

"Thinking of walking the other side?" Then Russell grimaced. "Sorry, forgot. Your ex. Not funny. Just come on through."

Josh found the fridge had two really smashing whites and he'd bet the cupboard had an exceptional red or twelve. Cassidy's reputation as a wine entrepreneur now surpassing her reputation as one of the nation's leading food-and-wine critics. Though they'd been friends for years, she still humbled the hell out of him. He took a Heineken.

The condo boasted such an amazing view out the window, ten stories up right on top of the hill overlooking the waterfront, that he didn't notice the apartment at first.

There was their ferry, already headed back across the water.

"Did that really happen?" he asked the empty living room.

The condo didn't answer.

If he were in any condition to judge, he'd say that he'd just had the best date of his life, but he knew he was still awash in the aftereffects of Melanie's final embrace and did his best to push the thought aside. He could still feel her kiss burning on his lips.

He was in so much trouble here.

When he finally focused back on the condo, it was almost a comedy. Clearly, it had been purchased and decorated by Cassidy. Her taste was elegant and understated: pale greens and soft golds set on a base of white carpet.

Except for a big, dark-blue recliner with a stack of books spilling off the table beside it. A very high-end camera dangled precariously from the edge of a low shelf.

Apparently the neck strap was too enticing for a small black cat with a ridiculous amount of hair for such a pristine apartment. It was deeply snarled in the strap, engaged in combat to the death. Josh managed to nudge the camera back to safety without strangling the cat.

Art covered the walls. Most of it was clearly Russell's photography, except for a line of small photos over the couch. A dozen pictures of sailboats and lighthouses—Cassidy's and Russell's year-long courtship captured for posterity. The last picture was of the two of them getting married at the Mukilteo Light. Josh remembered that; it had been a hell of a party. He'd gone with Constance and… Crap!

He shoved the memory aside and moved quickly out onto the balcony. There was a set of iron chairs and small side tables. Enough room for four guys to sit comfortably and watch the busy waterfront like gods on high. It was bright, the sun was shifting west though still a ways from setting. He kept his sunglasses on.

There were two guys there with Russell. He didn't know them, though one looked vaguely familiar.

"Angelo's cooking tonight. This one's Bill Cullen, Perrin's other half," Russell waved a hand at a man to match Josh's six feet, but he was a big-boned guy without an ounce of fat. Josh wouldn't want to wrestle him. A tall, lean, older man—more patrician—was introduced as, "Hogan Stanford who is still trying to prove he's worthy of Mama Maria."

"Six months since we were married, Russell. You have to let a fellow sailor into safe harbor sometime."

"No, I don't." By Russell's smug and relaxed attitude it was clear that he long since had. "Marrying Mama Maria is not a get into jail free card."

"A cell I plan to stay in forever."

"Good thing," Russell drank his beer, "or Angelo and I will have to kill you."

"C'mon man." Bill tossed in his own two cents. "You think Maria would leave even a tiny piece of him for us to kill off? Wouldn't happen. That woman is scary. She threatened me about treating Perrin right the first time we met. Actually threatened me." He shivered as if a chill had just washed over his soul.

"She made me breakfast the first time we met," Hogan looked immensely pleased.

Russell covered his ears, "Na-na-na-na. Don't want to be hearing that shit, man. Can't believe that Mama Maria slept with you on your first date. Just not right. Na-na-na-na."

By Hogan's grin, Josh could see that there was a web of half-truths that the man had been feeding Russell for some time, and would probably get away with continuing for some time more. That's when he figured out why Hogan was familiar.

"You're the shelter cook. Down in Pioneer Square."

"I am. Volunteer there five days a week. Why—oh, you're the early riser in Maria's building." Then Josh saw Hogan aim a wicked smile at Russell while he was looking out at the water. "Yep! I know that building well. Maria and I—"

Russell again covered his ears, "Na-na-na-na. Shit, Josh, don't encourage the man. To hear him tell it, they probably had sex on the kitchen floor. He and Mama Maria. Just such a bad image."

Hogan's suddenly soft smile indicated that may have just been the first fact Russell had gotten right.

Josh could get to like this. He settled into a chair between Russell and Hogan. This was exactly what he needed. A night with the boys to get his libido back in check.

Then Bill leaned forward to look at him around Russell, "I'd be careful, Josh. I hear Russell is even more protective of Melanie than he was of Maria."

"Sure," Russell nodded. "Melanie needs more protecting than Maria. But what does she have to do with this?" He went to take a drag on his beer.

Bill's smile was wicked, "Perrin says that Melanie and Josh here are shacking up together in Angelo and Maria's condo."

What the hell? Josh had never met him before and he was getting thrown under the bus by the man?

Russell choked on his beer, hacking and sending spray everywhere—over his jeans, even dribbling down his chin. "You what?!" he thundered loud enough to be heard on the ferry now halfway across the Sound.

Josh wondered if he was about to die from a ten-story fall.

Hogan tapped his beer bottle against the one Joshua had yet to raise to his lips, then leaned in and whispered as Russell continued to splutter, "Welcome to the club, my boy."

MELANIE ARRIVED at Cutters Crabhouse with her heart still skipping every third beat. She should have brought Joshua for support, but that wouldn't be appropriate. Besides, since when did Melanie need someone else's support? Still, a part of her admitted, his little pep talk about how she could do anything should give her heart. Did give her some. But would it be enough to face the *Fabulous Five?*

The bar was already hopping though it wasn't quite five o'clock yet. An upscale urban hangout with an amazing view of Pike Place Market and the southern Seattle waterfront, it would be packed and roaring with the after-work crowd within the hour. Her history in Seattle had been cluttered with this place.

Her first trip here had included a dinner with Russell in the main restaurant beyond the bar, set against one of the best views in all Seattle. That was back when— She shuddered from the thought and lost some of her confidence. That was the weekend she had fallen in love with him and then broken up with him. Her heart had been an impregnable fortress ever since...

Right up until Joshua. And she was too worried at the moment to decide whether or not he was somehow gaining entrance past that protection.

Her last visit had included lunch with Perrin, and it was where she'd first met Joshua. At that table, close by the window, now occupied by a pair of couples clearly enjoying themselves. She hadn't paid too much attention to him at that meal, but she would take strength from their having been here together, even in a group.

Though Melanie had arrived early, four of *The Fabulous Five* were already there. And waiting. She lurked a moment in the shadows, dropping her heart rate by sheer willpower as she assessed them. While she did so, she pulled out her French braid to let her hair flow free. She would find strength in arriving as Melanie the model. She finger-combed the worst of the twists free until it should billow properly. No time to retreat and brush it out.

The four women stood out in the chichi bar with its dark wood tables, tall chairs, and amazing view just beyond the glass. The afternoon sun streamed in through a softening screen and lit the four women so that they glowed like a runway show frozen in time.

Russell's wife Cassidy Knowles, the founder of the Wash-ington Wine Cooperative, already a major force in the national and international marketing of Puget Sound wines. She'd dressed in her classic black slacks and turtleneck, her russet hair spilling to her shoulders. They really needed to do an intervention and get some color into her wardrobe; she definitely had the figure for it.

Jo Parrano, who had married Angelo last fall, should have been a model. Her native-Alaskan dark hair and skin, and her voluptuous curves accented by one of Perrin's custom power suits clearly identified her as one of the most powerful women in Seattle.

Maria was dressed perfectly, as she always was. She understood color and flow. She was both beautiful and clearly the calm center, the true anchor of the group. If she could age the way Maria was, Melanie would be thrilled. It was patently ridiculous as Maria was almost a foot shorter than Melanie, but she was living proof that life began at fifty.

Perrin sat beside the still empty fifth chair and, as always, was a study in fashion. Her hair was golden rather than the dye jobs she used to sport. She wore a dress of jet-black velvet. It had one sleeve that started as a fingerless glove. At her shoulder, it broke into two waves that draped and cascaded down her slender figure so dramatically it would have made her face hard to focus on—the eyes just wanted to travel right down to the short slit-reveal at her calves. Except, the other shoulder and arm were bare and relieved the eye of its downward journey. Rather than losing the pale-skinned woman in the dramatic dress, she shone.

Who belonged in that empty fifth chair still eluded her. And where would she sit when she crossed the room? There should be a sixth seat. Unless she were being called in and dismissed for some reason.

Cassidy, Jo, and Perrin were obviously the original core group. Maria had joined in as much as a mother to the three grown women as a friend. And now all four were happily married to amazing men. Tamara, Perrin's new-adopted daughter, was too young to be the fifth. A great girl, but just a young teen. They were sitting in the bar at Cutters Crabhouse.

Well, she didn't need a mother. She was Melanie, she didn't need anyone. Joshua's face came to mind, but she ignored the thought.

Deep breath. Forge ahead.

She knew how to make an entrance. You executed the most powerful entrance by *not* making one. No grand gesture, no hard walk. Simply stroll naturally into the middle of the room, hesitate for just a second—not long enough to make you look uncertain, just enough to break the natural flow and catch the eye of anyone even partially looking in the right direction— then you hit the walk hard.

Melanie did it this time not to make the statement of her arrival and not to silence the crowded upscale bar perched over the waterfront. She did it because it was the woman she felt most secure being in public. Melanie the model always controlled any room she entered and she controlled it this time as well.

"Damn, girl, but you can really walk," Perrin beckoned her over for a hug. "I've tried to do that, just in my studio, but I always feel stupid."

"That probably means you're doing it *correctement*. It is a crafted walk designed to make other women sweat and men weep with desire. While it is not normal, at times I find it to be useful."

Maria glanced to either side of Melanie. She herself of course didn't turn to watch the effect she'd caused; though she could certainly hear just how slowly the conversations were returning.

"Well, you seem to do your job this time. A wide collection of stunned puppy looks." Then she smiled up at Melanie. "You must teach me how to do that, so that I can do it to Hogan."

Melanie liked Maria. And while she didn't need a mother,

the woman was unfailingly thoughtful. Her kindness ran even deeper than Cassidy's.

"I could not do that," Melanie tried not to look uncertain as she remained standing by the fifth chair. Who was the other person?

"Trade secret, huh?" Perrin sipped at a Cosmopolitan.

"*Non!* I don't want to kill Hogan. Maria, you are already the perfect embodiment of a woman. If you do anything more, it is sure to slay the poor man."

That won her a round of laughter, a blush from Maria, and gleeful agreement from the three younger women who clearly loved the older woman deeply.

"Who else is coming?" The fifth chair was making her nervous. She felt exposed. Was she indeed supposed to just stand all evening?

"No one," Maria reached out to take Melanie's hand and gave her a slight tug to sit between her and Perrin. "We were *The Fearsome Foursome*. Not anymore. The chair is yours."

Melanie's knees went weak, so it was good that the seat was vacant to settle into before she collapsed. *The Fabulous Five.* This wasn't some test or a setup for a future favor. No entry on the tally sheet.

This was a welcome.

She had thought her invitation to Perrin's wedding was merely thoughtful. But they were offering her so much more.

They were treating her as if she belonged among them.

Well, wasn't that just as surprising as all hell?

JOSH SURVIVED, but it was a close thing. He'd never quite understood the full significance of the phrase "steam coming out his ears" until Russell rounded on him.

Suddenly two hands as big as meat cleavers were inches

from his throat. Hogan pulled Josh back toward him for protection—or so he first thought. Instead, Hogan wrapped an arm around Josh's throat, not quite choking him.

"I've got him for you Russell. Go for it."

Josh didn't know whether to feel betrayed or terrified. Then he realized that Hogan's move had neatly blocked Russell's first instinct to simply strangle Josh with his bare hands.

"What do you mean, 'shacking up with Melanie'?"

"I—"

"Hey," Hogan cut off Josh's attempts to explain. "If you had Melanie—The Melanie—practically living with you, would you throw her out of your bed?"

Russell flinched as if he was the one who'd been struck. "I already did that to her," his voice was barely a whisper, but Josh heard it.

"You did?" Bill and Hogan echoed Josh's thoughts.

Russell Morgan… And Melanie…?

"Is that why she's so damn gun shy?" Josh could feel his own heat rising. "You slept with her and then threw her out?" That last wasn't all that much softer from Russell's first shout.

Russell tried a wry smile, but it came out looking sickly. "I didn't know what I was doing at the time, but, yeah, that's pretty much right. Except it was worse. Damn woman fell in love with me…*then* I threw her out."

Josh didn't know what to say. Should Melanie have told him? They'd shared a few amazing kisses and a hug he would remember for the rest of his life, but it wasn't as if he expected her to be a virgin. It was just a shock that he knew one of her former—lovers was too uncomfortable a word—guys. The fact that Russell looked more upset than Josh felt actually made him feel a little better.

Hogan got up and went into the apartment. He came back with a tumbler with three fingers of scotch in it and handed it to Russell who knocked it straight back.

"Hey," Josh tried to make it light, "where's mine? I'm the one who almost got killed here."

"Yes," Hogan acknowledged as he settled back into his chair without fetching another glass. "But he needs it more."

Josh looked back at Russell.

He really did look like hell.

———

"NACHOS? I haven't eaten nachos in years." Melanie looked at the spread of appetizers before them. The clams weren't fattening by themselves, but eating them without the focaccia bread, which was practically dripping with butter, would be a crime. The deep-fried calamari was popular with the table, though she'd never been a big fan of it. But nachos. She had a terribly ridiculous weak spot for nachos.

"It's okay," Perrin dipped a piece of the bread into the clam juices, bit off a chunk, and sighed happily as she bit in. "Nothing here has calories or fat. Not as long as we're all together. It's one of the rules."

Melanie could already feel that second glass of wine. She never drank two glasses. Hell, she never drank all of one. She tried closing one eye, then both. But the nachos were still there teasing her nose. She opened one eye; the others were watching her.

"You are all bad influences."

There was a small cheer and much pride displayed around the table. "Don't make us suffer alone!"

Melanie didn't. She dipped the crab nacho into the dish of fresh-made guacamole and decided she was going to have to marry the chef.

"So, how far along are you?"

"With what?" Melanie really hoped Perrin was asking about

her business. Even if Melanie hadn't told Perrin she was working on it, she really hoped that's what it was.

Perrin's eye roll informed Melanie that her hopes were dashed.

Jo and Cassidy looked perplexed, so no one was talking behind her back at least. Though Maria's smile looked far too knowing for her comfort.

Melanie looked back at Perrin and assessed the situation. Nope, no way out of it. So, she'd give a little.

"We spent the day taking a ferry over to Bainbridge Island for lunch."

"So, that's why you left my shop so fast," Perrin nodded and Melanie would leave her with the possession of that bit of misinformation. It had been embarrassing enough sharing a full panic attack with Joshua; she didn't intend to share it with the rest of the world.

"Wait!" Cassidy held up her hands. "Wait just a second." She leaned forward as far as she could without upsetting the table. "You and who?"

She opened her mouth but Perrin leapt in on her moment of hesitation.

"She's sleeping with Josh Harper."

"I am not!"

"You're both staying in Angelo's condo; so you're sleeping together. If you're doing that in separate beds, you need to have your head examined. He is majorly cute."

"He is not!"

All four women turned to her at her protest and she knew she was caught, because Joshua most definitely was cute on any woman's scale. Discretion apparently lay at the bottom of her now empty wine glass. Well, if she had put her foot in it, she might as well go all the way. With a shrug, she flicked her hair back over her shoulder.

"He's *not* cute." She pictured him standing by the ferry ramp, still watching her when she turned back to check. The afternoon sun had lit his dark hair like the finest walnut furniture. His face, the brightening of his smile as she'd turned to look back and found him still watching her. The way he made her feel.

"He's beautiful."

"ANSWER. THE. GOD. DAMNED. QUESTION." Russell's growl sounded positively feral. Great, Josh was caged on a high and narrow balcony with a guy Hulking-out to twice his already substantial size.

"Which God damned question?" No way he was going to make it easy for the man.

Russell's glare deepened, if that was possible. "Are you sleeping with her?"

"Not that it's any of your god damned business, but no."

Most of the anger-bloated Hulk went away, and the slightly sad man had returned. "Why not?"

"Why am I not sleeping with the woman you just threatened to kill me over? What kind of a stupid question is that, Russell?"

"My kind. Cassie's always telling me I'm an idiot, but Melanie's really special. I don't want anyone messing with her."

Joshua considered ramming Russell's words right back down his throat as he was obviously someone who'd obliterated his own rules.

Russell held up his hands in resignation.

"I know. Just don't go there. Let's just acknowledge that I was a goddamn idiot before I met Cassie and she straightened me out."

So, Josh didn't go there. That's what friends were for. Or at least what you did for someone who'd resisted killing you outright. He bought himself some time to think by going in to get a glass of scotch. After a moment's consideration, he grabbed three tumblers and brought back the bottle, refilling Russell's before he handed round the rest.

They all raised a toast to the setting sun and knocked it back, at least he and Russell did. Bill and Hogan showed a little more control and left some in their glasses.

"I'm not sleeping with her for a lot of reasons. One, I've only known her for about two days. Two, I don't want someone as amazing as her to be my 'rebound' girl from my divorce because she deserves better than that. Three, because she deserves better than me. And four, because she deserves someone who sees Melanie, not the supermodel, and I can't seem to get around that entirely because the woman is so bloody breathtaking. Happy now?"

Russell studied Josh long enough in silence for Josh to feel that his throat was dry, so he sipped his beer rather than risking a look for where the scotch bottle had gone.

Then Russell turned to consult Bill and Hogan who nodded in response.

"Shit!" Russell cursed softly. "I always thought you were a decent enough guy, Josh. Did you have to go and prove it so that I look like more of an idiot than I am?"

"Sure," Josh tapped his beer against Russell's empty scotch glass, then sat back to enjoy the view and the company. "What are friends for?"

"Oh," Perrin placed a hand over her heart. "Dreamy kiss on a ferry boat. I hadn't thought of that. I need to take Bill out on a ferry crossing and get a kiss that sounds that dreamy."

"I've always liked Josh," Cassidy started with a nod that probably continued far longer than she intended. She was looking distinctly blurred.

Melanie was fairly sure it wasn't only her own perception through several glasses of wine that was causing it. Cassidy herself had softened and mellowed, revealing the genuinely gentle woman she was at the core.

"He's a wonderful guy. Not as amazing as my Russell, but a good guy. Known him since forever and I always liked Josh. He's a good gu— Hey, Melanie?"

"What?"

Cassidy stopped nodding and came slightly back into focus. "You and Josh would make an amazing couple."

Perrin jabbed Cassidy in the arm, "Hello. Welcome to the conversation. Can you picture the dress I could make them?"

Jo shook her head, "No." She shook back her long mane of dark hair, even drunk her posture was upright and elegant.

Melanie suspected that nothing disturbed the woman's lawyerly manner.

"You can't get Josh to wear a dress. You have to make the dress for Melanie. Suit for Mr. Har-pe-ter," she interrupted herself with a ladylike hiccup. She found her water glass on her third attempt.

"I don't know," Perrin's smile said that she was clearly still the most coherent of the three, though maybe not by much. "Josh is so pretty. We could put him in the dress and Melanie in a suit."

"I," Melanie drew herself upright to protest the conversation going on without her. "I am not marrying anyone."

Cassidy, Jo, and Perrin ignored her.

Maria Parrano took her hand, drawing Melanie's attention. With a gentle pressure, she pulled Melanie close enough for her to speak softly despite the noise of the bar and the ongoing debate over Melanie's wedding day.

"You will, you know."

"Will what?" Melanie wondered if it was her or if Maria's

words made no particular sense. Melanie had switched over to water some time ago and was sure she was only a little tipsy.

Maria's eyes were perfectly clear. "Oh dear girl," Maria kissed her on each cheek. "You will make a beautiful couple."

———

MELANIE WASN'T sure who was leading who home. Cassidy lived only a few blocks up the hill and had offered her a spare bedroom. At some point after Maria's comment, Melanie had switched back to wine without quite noticing how.

She suspected that Cassidy had been more coherent than she appeared and filled Melanie's water glass with a refreshing white wine when she wasn't paying enough attention.

No matter, she had neither the energy nor the inclination to return to the Pioneer Square condo. Joshua would probably be there and she wanted a little distance from him, at least enough to stop herself from jumping him. Because after the four women... No. After her four friends poking and prodding her and talking about their own husbands, both the appreciated quirks and the not so appreciated, she was certainly feeling ready to jump one Mr. Joshua Har-pe-ter.

Somehow between them, she and Cassidy climbed the nighttime Seattle streets; the city still alive with music from bars, their doors open and people enjoying late night treats around little tables at sidewalk cafes. They made it into Cassidy's condo. She aimed Cassidy into the master bedroom, where Russell's soft snores indicated that he hadn't waited up.

Cassidy reappeared a moment later and handed her a big shirt to wear as a nightgown. Then she was gone and Melanie stood in the hall lit only by the few streetlights that could reach this high.

She washed her face and changed in the guest bath. She was glad to see that Cassidy had given her an oversized woman's t-shirt rather than one of Russell's. As they'd once been lovers, that would have been too strange.

Russell's fluffy black cat was waiting outside the bathroom door to inspect her when she emerged. Without really thinking, she reached down and scratched it between the ears eliciting a happy buzz. She snatched her hand back and the animal eyed her strangely.

"I'm not explaining to you why cats freak me out. Go away." Her hand itched where that photo shoot cat of her childhood had slashed at her. Melanie slipped into the guest room, making sure that the cat, however disappointed, ended up on the other side of the door when she closed it.

In the vague light, she spotted a chair and dropped her belongings onto it. She turned for the bed, a vague outline of white that was her sole concern. After tonight's excesses, and this afternoon's emotional upheaval courtesy of Mr. Joshua Har-pe-ter, she could sleep for a week.

That's what they'd called him for the entire rest of the evening, the memory made her giggle a bit.

A voice sounded out of the dark, "Please don't throw a suit-case at me."

"JOSHUA," Melanie's voice was a breathy whisper.

Josh reached to turn on the bedside light, but thought better of it. He'd woken in time to see Melanie's unmistakable silhouette slipping in the door, but not soon enough to be sure she was clothed. He was instantly sober. Or at least sober enough to not assume he was hallucinating.

"I shall go somewhere else. Back to the condo." He could hear her gathering her things.

He could also hear her exhaustion. "No. I'll go. I can sleep on the couch or something." He remembered in time that he wasn't wearing anything under the covers, so he stayed in place.

"Cassidy—" she said at the same moment he said, "Russell—" They both hesitated.

"You don't think it was some master plan?" she really did sound wiped out.

Joshua reached around on the floor and found his underwear. He slipped them on under the covers as surreptitiously as he could while he responded.

"I like Russell and Cassidy, but neither one is sufficiently sneaky. Perrin, maybe, except she'd have first made you a nightgown out of taffeta or something. Maria is definitely sneaky enough, but not Russell or Cassidy. So, I'll just count myself impossibly fortunate and burn some candles of thanks to our Lady of Chance." He started to get out of bed. "I'll go."

"No. I—" she stopped, but it didn't sound as if she was gathering her things either. They were both exhausted and both too considerate. Well, she was. His body's reaction would prove him to be a complete and total cad if she turned on a light before he could find his jeans.

At an impasse—he knew that she'd leave if he insisted on going and neither of them would sleep soon.

"Melanie, how about this? You climb in here and I'll behave. I will promise that you will remain completely safe. We'll just sleep."

"You're being ridiculous."

"No. Completely and unbelievably stupid considering how much you've been occupying my thoughts today, but a promise has been made and a promise will be kept. C'mon."

She hesitated for several long moments, then he saw the faint outline moving toward him, followed by a soft *Merde!* as she stumbled on the clothes he'd dumped on the floor before crawling into bed.

"Get in this side; it's already warm." He held up the covers and slid over to the far side as she took the covers.

He lay there having no idea what he'd been thinking. The woman of his fantasies now lay possibly naked a mere foot away. Everything he'd promised himself to not think about—insane pedestal and all. Each motion of the mattress and the sheets as she settled sent bolts of electricity rocketing through him.

And his fantasies were becoming an issue. The pin-up fantasy of the most beautiful woman he'd ever seen was fast being replaced by the flesh-and-blood one who had kissed him with such abandon on the ferry; the one who had kept him chastely entertained and intrigued through a long date to Bainbridge and back; the one he really wanted to get his hands on.

He had to get up.

Go to the couch.

Sleep on the floor.

Something.

Before he could force himself to go, she rolled toward him. In moments her head rested on his shoulder. Her body, thankfully clothed, lay along his or he would have lost all control—promise or not. One of her legs, not the least little bit clothed, draped over one of his.

"You're a good man, Josshhua." Now he heard the slur in her voice. And not the least trace of French in her speech. Maybe not drunk, but he'd guess pretty damn loose or she wouldn't have crawled in. That made her completely and totally out of bounds, whether or not she offered. No way was he taking advantage of her.

She settled in, draped an arm across him, and fell asleep with a soft sigh.

Now what in hell was he supposed to do?

CHAPTER 8

*M*elanie woke the way she normally did; one moment asleep, the next wide awake.

Wide awake and nestled in a man's arms.

Joshua. She didn't need the soft morning's light edging in around the closed curtains to know instantly it was him. If felt as if they'd always slept together.

By the rise and fall of his chest, she knew he was asleep. One hand wrapped around her back, the other one resting on her hand which in turn rested on his chest. She had crawled in and curled up against him—what a total Jersey Shore hussy.

Except she didn't feel like one. Instead she felt like a woman who had her best night's sleep in recent memory while nestled safely in her lover's arms. Though he wasn't her lover.

She'd certainly never slept with a man without having sex before. Was something wrong with him? With her?

His chest slowly rose and fell several times before she remembered what he'd said. She'd been very tipsy, okay, soused, and half-passed out on her feet. Then Joshua had promised she'd be safe. Those were not words that any man had ever offered to her. Especially not offered and meant. Actually, no one had *ever* offered her safety, including her own mother.

And then he'd given her the warm side of the bed when she'd been chilled from the walk through cool night wind off the Sound.

She'd not only been safe, but felt safe. Exactly as he'd promised.

She considered making him break that promise right now. But they were guests in someone else's apartment. In Russell's! If someone had told her before last night that she'd ever sleep in Russell's home again, she'd have laughed in their face. She absolutely wasn't going to have sex here, no matter how incredible Joshua felt.

She managed to slip from his arms, gather her things, and make it to the guest bathroom with no one the wiser. Dressed, hair brushed, and face fresh scrubbed—she never wore makeup except on a shoot—ten minutes later she entered the kitchen.

Cassidy was sitting at the kitchen counter with a big mug of coffee and her computer tablet, though she didn't appear to be focusing well.

"Hi."

"Uh, hi," Cassidy looked up at her. "How in the hell can you look so together when my head feels like mush?"

"No hangover. Whatever wine you slipped me, it must have been the best quality."

"Actually," Cassidy wrapped her hands around her coffee mug like gripping a lifeline. "I think that was Jo. She appears all demure, but in truth she's very sneaky. You've got to watch that woman like a hawk. My mistake was letting Perrin switch me over to Cosmos. Help yourself to coffee."

"You really don't look like you slept much." Melanie took her time about making a cup of tea instead, moving softly in sympathy for Cassidy's condition. Espresso from French roast was among the French habits she'd never learned to enjoy.

"Russell greeted me very nicely—" Then Cassidy blushed hard and looked aside. "Sorry. Too much information. I know. I just—"

Melanie rested a hand on Cassidy's arm to stop her. "Russell and I were lovers. It didn't take, for many and valid reasons. He married you and loves you. Let us simply leave it at that. *N'est-ce pas?*"

Cassidy did her head nod thing again, nodding a couple too many times.

"You know. I think that's the first French you've spoken since last night," she squinted her eyes as if concentrating. "Maybe not even then. It fits you. You sound uptown New York."

Melanie blinked in surprise. How had she been so relaxed to let down her shields? Last night, too? She thought back, but couldn't be sure. What she did remember was immensely enjoying her inclusion in *The Fabulous Five*. And she couldn't feel the slightest sense of an entry on her internal tally sheet. She'd simply been welcome, just for herself. That too was a new experience.

"Joshua said the same thing, but he is a man, I'm not about to trust a man on such things."

"Like I think I said last night, Josh is a good guy. I've known him forever, since before he met his wife back when we were both upstart restaurant reviewers. Just friends, no spark there, then he met Constance. Who wasn't so constant. God I'm rambling. If this coffee cup were bigger, I'd just put my face in it."

"Maybe I should start trusting Joshua," Melanie topped up Cassidy's coffee. Then she decided that if her instincts were relaxed enough to drop her accent around Cassidy that just maybe she should trust that feeling all the more. "Besides, he also greeted me very nicely last night, if a little bit differently."

"Joshua?"

"He's asleep in your guest bedroom."

"Joshua?" Cassidy was blinking hard trying to get her brain going. "Josh!? I sent you to bed with Josh? Oh my God! I'm so *sorry*. It wasn't planned. I swear it wasn't. I—"

Melanie had to laugh. It really was too funny. Joshua had been absolutely right. Russell and Cassidy were sincere friends, but not conniving ones.

Melanie sat down across the counter and told her new friend about how her evening had ended.

JOSHUA SLEPT LATE into the morning and woke to the smell of frying bacon and coffee. He dragged on jeans and a t-shirt before padding out into the kitchen to find Russell battling the stove like a ship's cook on a stormy sea.

"Shit, Russell. You look worse than I feel."

"Yeah. You sleep okay?" Russell tossed in some more bacon and nodded toward the coffeemaker.

That's when Josh remembered.

He spun to look around but there were only the two of them. None of Melanie's things had been in the bedroom. He doubled back to check. Nothing. Gone as if it had never happened.

But it had. The other pillow was dented, the covers were mussed on both sides of the bed. Her pink bag from the dress shop was gone.

The memories were slowly returning through his foggy brain. He'd held her for hours, imagining what it might be like to do so every night. He'd buried his nose in her hair for a long time—long enough to actually sober up—just in case he never had a chance like that again. His idea of heaven had been wholly redefined by simply holding a sleeping woman.

"Huh," he looked around the condo again as he returned to

join Russell in the kitchen. She was definitely gone. Without waking him. Now what did that mean? "I slept great."

Josh made eggs and toast while Russell brought the bacon in for a landing. They took their plates to the balcony high above the bustle of a Pike Place Market morning.

CHAPTER 9

*M*elanie was determined. For the first time in days, maybe weeks, she felt as if she had Things to Do. Much more her natural state; she first went back to the Pioneer Square condo to change into her exercise clothes and do a virtuous workout.

She padded into the great room, cool and dim with the indirect morning light through the western windows. She liked that Maria and Angelo had left much of the main space open. Clearly, they'd only really cared about the kitchen. Even the dining table wasn't much. They probably planned to only test recipes here; any entertaining would be at the restaurant. A couch and a couple of big chairs were all that defined the living room. A television sat off to the side, not at a comfortable angle to any of the furniture, so that too was mostly unused.

It left her a large expanse of gleaming bare wood. From her point of view it was perfect. It gave a six-foot tall woman room to do her yoga stretches without fear of running into furniture or inopportune sections of wall. She'd become lax since the loss of the swimsuit photo shoot. In just one week she could feel the loss of flexibility and tone.

That would never do. She did a double session until a sheen of sweat made it hazardous to continue until she had the chance to purchase a mat. Carlo's hotel room had a large oriental carpet that worked well, but this expanse of shining oak was a slipping risk.

She almost didn't want to shower. When she did, she'd lose that scent of Joshua that...wasn't clinging to her so much as following her around. A pleasant companion.

But she had things to do, so into the shower she went. She grabbed the last bowl of Joshua's minestrone soup for lunch, thanking him with each luscious spoonful. She considered feeling guilty about eating it without asking first. But if she wasn't going to feel guilty for sleeping with the man, she wasn't going to feel guilty for finishing his soup.

And she certainly didn't. Cassidy had sighed romantically when Melanie recounted how Josh had declared she'd be safe, then delivered on that promise.

"I wouldn't tempt him again though. You'd risk ruining a perfect story." Cassidy had looked serious, as if the story was the most important part. Well, maybe it was. Josh was a writer; he would understand the importance of careful beginnings.

Melanie had walked halfway up the First Avenue hill, opening an effortless path through the Seattle crowd with just a small dose of New York attitude, when she stumbled to a halt. If she'd stopped on a sidewalk in New York she'd have been trampled—you broke the Big Apple's pedestrian flow at your own risk. In Seattle, one person bumped her lightly and immediately apologized.

What had ground her to a halt was that word "beginnings." She'd selected lovers, knowing that's all they were. She'd fallen in love with only one of them. Dear Russell had also thought they were simply two people who enjoyed each other and the sensation they created on the New York scene. She was the one who'd broken that bargain and fallen for him. But their "beginning" had been like any other.

A party. Did she remember whose?

A passing brush on her shoulder got her moving again, though more slowly than before.

It was the meet-and-greet party for her second season on the swimsuit photo shoot. He'd been handsome, charming, and acting very single. Melanie had googled him to make sure, leaving the other girls to fawn over one of the handsomest men she'd ever seen. He was indeed single. It was buried fairly deep, but she also found that he was a billionaire's son as well as owning his own photo studio.

That had caught her attention, but with a second shoot under her belt—and she hadn't known it yet, but her first cover as well—she wasn't doing badly herself. He'd hooked up with another of the models who knew nothing about him, and that had been fine.

Whatever else Russell did or however he acted at parties, behind the camera he was both professional and masterful. He drew the absolute best out of his models. He had done the simplest things, which evoked emotions inside her that she didn't know were there—buried or otherwise. After a session with Russell Morgan, a girl needed a cold shower simply to think clearly. He made it easy to lose herself in the role of sexual goddess; he made her believe it of herself.

But their eventual "beginning" had been like any other of her affairs. More intriguing, more artfully played, more fun, but not so notably different. He'd dragged it out over a year: a chance meeting here, hiring her for a small ad shoot there, finding out that he'd referred her to a shoot with an up-and-coming designer that no one had heard of but had then burst onto the scene.

Then he'd taken her to lunch...and to bed. Or perhaps she'd done the taking. It had been as mutual as it had been expected.

But with Joshua she already had stories and promises and steamy kisses. *Merde!* They'd slept together and held each other through the night, not like *lovers*, but like she imagined people *in love* did.

She'd never had a real beginning even as a teen. At the time she'd discovered boys, or rather boys had discovered her, she'd been foolish and naïve, giving up her first kiss before her first handholding, her virginity for empty words. She'd wised up fast and remained that way ever since.

Melanie didn't feel wise around Joshua; she felt...

Again she stopped in the middle of the sidewalk, blinking in surprise to find herself outside of Perrin's Glorious Garb with no memory of the last half dozen blocks. It was a wonder she hadn't been killed in traffic crossing the street.

Around Joshua she felt... Still the word eluded her.

Melanie smiled to herself as she entered the shop, the doorbell jingling brightly.

Maybe tonight she'd find out just how Joshua made her feel. She'd wager it would be *incroyable* and was a little surprised at how eager she was to win that bet.

"You want me to what?" Joshua shook his head. "No way."

"C'mon man," Angelo leaned forward over the plate of Baci —hazelnut and chocolate "kisses" Maria had made this morning—that they'd been pillaging since lunch. "I'll even... I'll even—"

"He'll even pay you," Russell nursed an iced tea, looking a little less gray and bleary-eyed than he had this morning.

Now it was Angelo's turn to turn a bit gray, but he nodded.

"No," Joshua shook his head. "First, you can't go on feeding me gratis no matter how damn much I'm enjoying it. Second, I don't want to write any more food articles."

Russell slapped the table, and then winced showing his hangover was not wholly cleared.

"That's it," he continued in a softer voice. "You don't do this and Angelo cuts you off. You write for him; he goes on feeding you guilt free."

"But I don't want to write any more of that—"

"Don't say it," Russell stopped him suddenly clear-eyed.

Joshua glared at him.

"I did that for a while, called my photography crap because it wasn't what I thought it should be. I'd look at a Bourke-White print, and then my latest spread for Prada and feel like a total sell-out. But I've learned that I'm damn good at what I do. Don't call your art crap. You really don't want to do it? Fine. You're an idiot, but fine. But just from one artist to another, don't put it down."

"Why the hell am I an idiot?"

"You're staying in the same condo as Melanie. Have you at least kissed her yet?"

"I have." But no way was he going to tell Russell that there'd been more than that. Especially not that they'd slept together in his own condo.

"Okay," Russell sighed a bit sadly. "At least you're not a complete idiot."

Joshua would keep his thoughts on that point to himself.

"Write Angelo's press release," Russell made it a suggestion. "Give it the pizzazz that I can't seem to find on this one. You get to keep eating Angelo's fucking awesome food."

"Damn straight you call it that," Angelo pitched in.

"And the words might prime the pump a bit. Maybe it gets your novel moving because it sure isn't doing squat now, is it?"

"How did you know?" It wasn't—not even a little—but he hadn't been advertising that.

Russell simply looked at him steadily.

"Crap! I didn't think it showed that badly."

"It shows, buddy. So say you'll write the damn thing. Then you can tell us about when you kissed Melanie and why you didn't mention a breath of it last night."

"PERRIN," Melanie traded a surprisingly warm hug with Perrin back in the workroom of her shop. "I actually wanted to talk to you about something different last night, but never got around to it."

"About you making it with Josh?"

"No," Melanie sighed. She doubted that Cassidy would have called Perrin to spread the news of last night's adventure, but somehow the story of last night had traveled. Perhaps these three women were telepathic with each other.

"Can't blame a girl for trying?"

That's when Melanie noticed the fabrics Perrin was working with today. A pure silk Duchesse satin that breathed with the faintest pearlescent sheen and a medium-weight silk crepe back satin in the palest, most perfect sky blue. She couldn't stop herself from reaching out to stroke the materials.

"Soft, huh?"

"Oh my god, Perrin. Aren't these like forty dollars a yard?"

"Fifty and fifty-five, wholesale. Sometimes a dress calls for the absolute best."

"Well, it is a lucky woman who will be wearing this dress."

"She won't let me help her even measure it," Tamara came in and dropped her school bag under the counter. She was a sharp contrast to her new mother, dark curly hair flowing to her shoulders versus Perrin's short golden blonde. Their skin was a sharp contrast as well, Tamara a permanent sun-kissed gold and Perrin almost as pale as the silk spread across the table.

Perrin hugged Tamara hard in greeting and Melanie was glad to see it was fully returned. She felt a dozen different pulls inside. The pull of a mother and daughter who clearly loved one another and were happier together than apart, the exact opposite of her own maternal relationship. And the pull of mother with child. Melanie had never pictured herself with a child, but watching the two of them together, she could almost see it.

"You," Perrin leaned down to kiss Tamara on top of the head before letting her go, "can spend the afternoon on a project here if you promise to do your homework tonight."

Tamara offered an indifferent shrug, exactly as you'd expect from a teen.

Perrin winked at Melanie before continuing. "Because today you have a clothing line to start designing."

"I do?" Any affectation of disinterest evaporated in that instant.

Melanie did her best to hide her smile, but sliding on her model shield couldn't suppress it. Tamara's eyes had gone saucer wide.

"Yes. I showed your sketches to one of the best professionals in the business," Perrin smiled at Melanie.

Tamara's jaw dropped as she turned to face Melanie for a moment then turned back to look up at her mom.

"And she said that they were a great start, really pretty, and you needed your own youth line. You get to name it, brand it, and design it. I'll help you with all of that and the business."

"TJPW!" she blurted out. "That's what it's called. Tam, Jasp— my little brother is named Jaspar," Tammy told Melanie as if they didn't already know each other. "P is for Perrin, and W for dad. I know. I know. Everyone calls him Bill. I thought about TJBP and got an oil company, the other way around I got Peanut Butter, so he gets W for William. The weird acronym will be cool. I've got a design for the logo at home. I really get my own line?" At the last she went from an effervescent rush back to breathy disbelief.

At Perrin's nod, the girl leapt into Perrin's arms.

Melanie had to look away from the sheer power of such joy. What might she have become with even that little bit of encouragement?

A gentle touch on her arm drew her attention back. Tamara stood close beside her. She mouthed a silent thank you and hugged Melanie gently. Melanie returned it the best she knew how.

Then, with a cry, "There's so much to do!" Tamara turned back into a thirteen-year-old whirlwind, digging a sketchbook out of her pack and flipping to pages filled with more sketches than the ones that had been in the sample. Without hesitation, she moved to the fabric wall, grabbed a pair of scissors, and began trimming samples off the corners of an assortment of colors and materials to tape down beside her designs.

Perrin leaned in close to Melanie and added a kiss on each cheek to add to Tamara's thanks. "So much to do, she isn't kidding."

"That's what I wanted to talk to you about," Melanie had thought the moment had eluded her again, but instead it had returned reinforced. The time was now.

When Melanie pulled out the file folder of letters and e-mails, Perrin grimaced. Then, she sat on the stool beside Melanie, close enough that their knees were brushing. Melanie was reminded of her lunch with Joshua and let that help her confidence.

"Okay," Perrin took a deep breath and tried to offer her a smile. "Okay. How do I survive what's happening to me?"

"*Bon.* At least you see the problem." Melanie pulled out her notebook that she'd worked on at Elliot Bay Bookstore and Joshua's notes of a few strategic enhancements.

CHAPTER 10

"*What* are you working on? And what is that divine smell?"

Joshua jerked back up from typing, inhaling like a diver emerging from the depths after his air tank had run out. Once again he'd missed Melanie's entry into the condo.

He could only watch in stunned amazement as she crossed from the front door over to where he was set up on the dining table. She always walked like magic, every motion was a joy. But there was something more today. A lightness in her step, the damn woman shone like the springtime outside.

That she came directly to him and hit him with a kiss as powerful as any Taser, left him stunned speechless.

"Joshua? Melanie to Joshua? Hello. Anyone there?"

"Uh-uh." Definitely not. He didn't trust himself to try words yet, even mustering up a grunt was a hard-won victory.

She moved over to inspect the oven. His eyes continued to track her even if his brain couldn't. He knew he was reacting badly, like some gobsmacked schoolboy, but he couldn't stop.

One of the most beautiful women on the planet had just greeted him as if they hadn't spent last night curled up together.

Or rather she greeted him as if that's exactly what they'd done. He still couldn't believe it.

She squatted down and eased open the oven to peek. It was a fluid motion that sent heat rippling along his body. His mouth had gone dry and neither swallowing hard nor taking a slug from the long since gone warm lemonade sitting beside his computer helped in the slightest.

"It's," he managed in a lame croak. "It's lasagna."

She turned to grimace at him, then tried to cover it for his sake.

"No. Not carb-laden pasta. Instead I used thin slices of roasted eggplant, low fat cheeses, and homemade red sauce. There's a tossed salad in the fridge, just needs some avocado sliced over it right before I serve it."

"Oh my God, that sounds amazing." Melanie flowed back to the table.

"I…" his pulse jumped significantly as she settled in the closest chair. "I cheated. I used Angelo's red sauce, mine takes a couple days to meld flavors properly. So does his, but he always has a large batch of it going. I actually stole his recipe." Babbling again. Since last night, her smell was such a part of his memory that he could pick it out despite the aromatic kitchen.

"What are you working on?"

"An article for Angelo. Did you have a good day?" *Do you have any idea how constantly I was thinking about you?*

"I did. I sat with Perrin and showed her the business plan we wrote up. It took away some of her fear, but she hasn't bought in the whole way yet. Which is not a terrible thing. The plan is still very rough and she has more than enough common sense to see that. I'm not sure what is missing, but we made progress."

Joshua nodded and tried some more lemonade.

Melanie smiled at him coyly.

Joshua tried to remember how to breathe, because his autonomic systems had just shut down.

"It would be a shame to waste such a meal."

"Waste? Why would it be wasted?"

Melanie took his hand and pulled him easily to his feet.

He stumbled after her as she returned to the kitchen, leading him like a puppy on a leash.

She turned off the oven and the timer. Then she led him toward the bedroom. Her bedroom.

"No. Wait. No!" His brain finally cut back in and he dug in his heels, her fingers almost slipping from his.

She looked at him in surprise, "Don't you want this?"

"Like I want a glass of Côtes de Rhône after eating Robuchon's Steak au Poivre," Josh swallowed again. "That means yes, desperately. But you don't want me."

"How do you know what I'm thinking?"

"Oh. Okay, I don't. I'll admit that."

"Excellent," she tugged on his hand, but he resisted.

"You don't want me. No, scratch that. Speaking for you again. I. Me. I don't want to do this."

"And yet you said, *Oui, désespérément.*"

"And I meant it." He pulled his fingers from her grasp so that he stood some chance of thinking coherently. "But I'm a mess."

"So you keep assuring me. And I'm not any better. I simply know that I want you in my bed and you are now the first man to ever tell me no."

She reached for him, but he backed off. Dragging his hands through his hair did nothing to help.

"Melanie," he tried to sound calm and rational. "I don't want you as my rebound lover. I don't want to bring my feelings of hurt and betrayal from my ex-wife into your bed. You deserve so much more than that. So much more than...me."

Melanie laughed at him. She actually laughed at him. "Cassidy was so right about you."

"Cassidy? What does she have to do with this?"

"She said," Melanie took his hand again and once more led

him, "that you were one of the most decent and *charmant* men she'd ever met. She was right." She stopped just inside the bedroom and closed the door behind them.

He felt as if he was now on the wrong side of the bars around a lion's cage. Lioness' cage.

"Joshua, just answer me one question. Honestly."

He looked into that perfect blue of her eyes and nodded, "Always. That's what I'm trying to do is be hone—"

"Shh," she rested a finger across his lips. "One word answer: yes or no. Okay?"

He nodded, not wanting her to remove her finger.

"Do you want to be with me?"

"Gods yes. So much—"

"One word, Joshua." Her laugh sparked his own smile to life. "Just one, Mr. Writer."

There was only one answer to the question. He pulled her into his arms, buried his face in her hair and crushed her against him. He held her so tightly that he'd escape.

MELANIE HAD NEVER MET such a man. He didn't grab, grope, pinch, didn't even kiss her. For a moment she half feared it might be a hug and then a "no." But it wasn't. It was a man holding her so close simply because he wanted to. As if the holding was more important than the lovemaking. It was, but no man ever understood that.

In turn, she simply wrapped her arms around his neck, rested her head on his shoulder and hung on. A gentle swaying motion came over them, building to a slow dance in which their bodies rubbed, nestled, warmed, heated, and finally burned.

When at last he kissed her, any sign of the gentle lover had vanished. Joshua was replaced by a man with need. *Désespérément* indeed. His hands roved over her, not grabbing, but rather studying, learning, memorizing. Such strong hands, as if custom-made to appreciate a woman's shape. Her shape.

Though the bed was a bare two steps away, that was too far. He pushed her against the door as she wrapped herself about him. Most men were too rough, and she had to warn them to take care as she bruised easily. Not Joshua. Without holding back, he perfectly judged where pleasure soared without harm.

Except that his kiss was overwhelmingly powerful. For all he was doing to her body, their kiss had yet to end. He swallowed her purr of raw pleasure and his deep-throated moan in response vibrated right down her body.

She had unleashed the wild beast inside the gentle man.

Melanie gave herself to him to be consumed.

JOSH FELT the moment of change. He wasn't sure from which of them it had come, but it was change. One moment he'd been holding Melanie the gorgeous supermodel. The next he'd been holding a woman with no name; not that she was nameless or faceless, but rather that no single name could describe her or contain such a person. A woman who offered her very being for him to hold, to discover, to revel in. A woman who embodied desire and passion and joy.

He lost himself as well. There was no Josh. There was only a man who wanted to bring this woman pleasure like none she'd ever imagined. There would be no tender moment. Not this time. The need was too great, as if they were male and female genders personified and all passion, heat, and fire of the species must be expressed only through them.

At times she whimpered, at times he did. Clothing was shed or torn aside. There would be time to marvel at such skin, such curves later. Now there was only hunger. Beyond sex, beyond need, beyond desperation. Their bodies knew what they themselves couldn't possibly. They simply belonged together in a state like none he'd ever tread before.

Somehow, somewhere, they stumbled to the bed and found protection. And when she took him from above, when she arched her head back and her hair had showered over her like sunlight, he wanted to unleash a cry of triumph that would rattle off the very heavens.

MELANIE HAD DIED. She knew it for a fact. And she had slaughtered the best lover she'd ever had. She lay upon the chest of the dead man and listened to his heart continue to hammer just as hers did. She'd never felt such a release, had never so lost herself to the act of sex.

She almost blushed at the thought. Calling what they had just done "sex" was like calling Josh's gourmet eggplant lasagna a Stouffers frozen dinner.

When making love, Melanie always retained control, maintained command. Even when appearing submissive, she still stood a half-step aside to monitor, shift, or shape the moment. Not this time. *Dieu!* Not anywhere close to control. She'd thrashed like a wild woman, taking everything he could give and begging for more.

And now they were both dead. Had to be after that.

Impossibly, showing a muscle control she knew she lacked, Joshua placed a hand on her back and began slowly stroking up and down her spine. As he went, she could feel him slowly sorting her hair from the tangle it must be, finger-combing it back to some sense of order. They must still be alive. Heaven, even if it felt this *incroyable*, would never include Melanie having tangled hair. So they must still be alive. On Earth.

"There's no way we can ever repeat that." She tried not to

feel sad at the thought. She was glad to have been there even once.

He kissed the top of her head. "Maybe not, but we can sure try."

She nodded. That was encouraging.

THEY ATE A SILENT, candlelit dinner. Words would be too much, too big. Joshua had pulled on jeans without underwear, and Melanie had slid into an overlarge t-shirt that kept sliding off one of her shoulders. She kept pulling it back into place so that she could watch Joshua's eyes go dark with heat each time it slid off again.

The only thing that kept her from completely fawning over the food was that if she started to talk about the amazing food, then she'd give voice to the incredible sex. And she liked that a man so full of words wasn't able to speak in her presence.

But the pressure of the silence built. Finally it grew until it wrapped so thick and warm between them that it filled the condo wall-to-wall, floor-to-ceiling.

She set down her plate, removed his from his nerveless hands and set it on the table.

He didn't move. He simply looked up at her with those wide dark eyes.

She straddled him in the chair and held on as he took her once again. This time with all the care and tenderness that had been lacking before. Their need had gone quiet and careful. The candlelight caught highlights in his hair, glimmered in his eyes, and made her feel understood and welcome.

He leaned her back to gain access to her chest. She rested her back on the rounded table's edge, dug her fingers into his soft hair and hung on. He murmured his appreciation as he sucked the warmth, heating her chest, until it flooded over her and all she could do was hold him tight to her as her world shifted.

Joshua was not some casual lover. This was not a night of shared sex and a few weeks or months later, *c'est la vie.* She'd always thought the phrase "life-changing sex" to be a naïve and unlikely phrase. Even if this sex didn't change her life, it had certainly tossed out any previous standard she'd ever had.

When they'd both gone over the top as quietly this time as they'd roared over it before, they didn't move. Joshua held her in his lap, resting his head on her shoulder, her own cheek on the top of his impossibly soft hair.

"So," she whispered, just loud enough to be heard over the distant jazz music coming in through the open kitchen window. "Are you going to resist me in the future?"

"I don't know why I was dumb enough to try the first time. Your slightest whim is my command."

"Well, there is this flower that only grows in ancient Tibet—"

Joshua groaned, "I'll wager that going there will not turn me into Batman, which is a pity. I've always lusted after his car."

Melanie rewarded him with a kiss atop his head for understanding her joke. She'd gone to the movie to see Christian Bale, he was ever so enjoyable to look at. She used to do that, make obscure comments, but no one ever understood. It made people uncomfortable, including her. But Joshua consistently understood her obscure asides. One more piece of herself that she could be around him.

"Okay. Here I have for you *une question* that you have carefully avoided every single time I've asked. This time, you have to answer it." It was fun to tease him with the French model, especially because he saw the real Melanie so clearly.

She could feel his nod against her chest. The motion almost made her drag him back to bed. It was so close and personal.

"What are you writing, and why is it making you so *très misérable?*"

"WHAT MAKES YOU THINK—" Josh didn't bother finishing the question. Even Russell had caught on that he was unhappy with his writing, which meant he was being pretty damned obvious about it.

He shifted so that his face was turned directly into Melanie's shoulder. It felt as if he could hide there. Her well-defined collarbone lined up with the bridge of his nose. His nose snuggled into the softness of the muscle just below, his lips on the first suggestion of the rise of her breast. She still rested her cheek atop his head and he could feel her hair sliding over his arms and bare back like a cloak of safety.

"I've had this idea since forever. A foodie mystery. Hercule Poirot meets, I don't know, Julia Child. But every time I try writing, it just sounds contrived or pompous. I write, wrote for a living. And now I'm wondering if I should get my old job back." Had Shirene already contacted Elric? Yes, he'd left New York and quit the magazine almost two weeks ago and she had a magazine to run. She'd probably hung up the phone with him and speed dialed Elric. No call back for other suggestions probably meant he'd leapt at the opportunity as predicted.

Melanie didn't say anything. He'd seen her in the bookstore at Bainbridge. He knew she was an avid reader. Maybe she was thinking what an idiot he was to imagine he could jump from journalism to novel-length fiction.

"I tried opening with a punch like you suggested, but since I don't know what I'm punching, it just comes out lame. Angelo and Russell cooked up this deal where I'm writing him a set of marketing press releases and website copy for the restaurant. A phased campaign. He's thinking about a third restaurant but wants to build up some attention beforehand."

"It is sidetracking you from your novel?"

Melanie smelled so spectacular. He ran one hand up her

back beneath the t-shirt, again appreciating her deceptive strength. His other arm remained cinched about her waist to anchor her securely in his lap.

"I see. I am the one sidetracking your attention."

"Perhaps tonight a little more than usual," he admitted. His hands, his senses, his brain was reeling from the floodgates this woman had opened inside him. "Not that I'm complaining."

"Nor I," and she made a motion with her hips that took his breath away. Then she shifted out of his arms until she was once again sitting across from him. She stretched out her forever-long legs, the tail of her t-shirt hiding almost none of their glorious length—or much of anything else—and rested them on his knee.

He began massaging her feet.

"But that is not answering my question again, *monsieur*. And that will never do. Tell me of your story."

Again the image of the lioness struck him. The deadly, powerful, beautiful queen of the savannah, with the power to transform herself into passionate lover, or abandon herself to the moment.

"That's the problem. I don't have one."

"Okay, tell me of your characters."

"They're all bland, or flat, or... Hell, I don't know!"

Melanie closed her eyes as he found a knot down in the arch of her foot. Her breathing picked up pace a bit, her breasts lifting enticingly against the loose, worn-thin Michael Kors t-shirt.

"Oh," she breathed when the muscle had loosened up and he'd eased off. "If you ever want anything from me. Sex, personal shopping, someone to order takeout, just do that again."

He'd have to remember that. He didn't think it would be hard to recall. He was well into the other foot by the time she spoke again.

"Maybe your problem is like a runway show."

He couldn't imagine how, but was glad to listen. She could read the *Wall Street Journal*, all of it, and he'd be glad to listen to her voice. Especially if she was wearing nothing but that thin t-shirt.

"You are starting with the finished show."

"Huh? What? No I'm not. I've got nothing finished. I haven't written a single paragraph worth saving." He forced his gaze up from her amazing breasts to her amused eyes.

"You are starting with the show. A designer never begins with a show. They start with a piece: a jacket, a dress, or..." she wiggled a toe against his ribs which tickled, "...or an emotion. Then another. It is only then that they can build an entire outfit, when they have found the unique qualities of all of those pieces."

"Then you have a show."

"Silly man," she rubbed a foot along his leg, impossibly eliciting a response from his body that he'd have bet was long past recovery. "Then you have one outfit. A twelve-outfit show can easily take twenty or thirty outfits to discover, for some designers it can take hundreds to put together a twenty-piece fall line. Then, it must all be in the right order. Do you write reviews?"

"Sure."

"*Non!* You write about a restaurant, you set it in a city, perhaps a neighborhood. Then you tell the story of its ambience. You might give a hint of a dish as a tease, but you do not describe the whole dish at once. That is for later, to be discovered by the reader as they wind through your review. That is why I like your reviews so much."

Josh had to fight down the distinct urge to preen a bit at the compliment. However he could see what she was after and it made sense. He went to speak, but Melanie was on a roll, sitting up, leaning forward, her feet now on the floor.

"You think I just walk. Any girl can just walk. It is all most girls do is walk. Look, I show you."

Oddly, with this different kind of impatience she didn't slip back into New Jersey, but actually back into her model-world French. No, it wasn't impatience or anger. That's why. It was excitement.

She jumped to her feet. "This walk. The *Grand Pas*, 'Big Stride.' This one. Watch the walk, not me." She set off across the living room with a hard punch that made the t-shirt flounce and bounce in an interesting way, but did look a bit ridiculous.

"Or this one!" Her abrupt tone forced his attention wholly onto the walk. A purposeful stride, more appropriate to a power suit at a Fortune 100 meeting than a t-shirt in a condo.

She continued back and forth, showing him a dozen walks or more, each so unique he could still identify them, even if he didn't know how she did it. Each as unique as a character. She started giving them names. Veronica was practically a street-walker. Jessie clearly wore a tennis skirt. Razz would be in leather and chains and was so smokin' hot that he wouldn't mind running into her a time or two.

"This one. Her name is Kate. A new fashion editor I have only met a few times. She is a powerful woman, if a little unsure of herself. She shows that to no one. But there is a tiny slice of it that only the right man can see, that least bit of vulnerability." And she walked away from him with a near perfect, almost military confidence. Three steps from the front door, she half turned to look back over her shoulder, but didn't quite finish the turn. Just that flash of uncertainty totally changing the character. An eyeblink and he would have missed it. If she hadn't told him, he'd certainly have caught the feeling though not why he felt it.

Melanie stood at the far side of the room, her fists on her hips. "*Oui?*"

"*Oui,*" she was absolutely right. He was trying to write a

novel. He needed to write a character first, after that maybe a scene.

Then Melanie came walking straight toward him rather than up and down the length of the room. She walked with a perfect awareness of how the t-shirt skimmed the top of her thighs, shrugged the t-shirt off one shoulder at just the right moment to jack his libido through the roof. Head down. Enough tilt for her face and chest to be wholly hidden by her swinging hair, forcing all attention to her legs and hips. She let each leg carry her weight in turn and her hips completely relax. It caused them to sway in a way that was making him sweat.

She strode up then halted abruptly, her knees a breath away from his. Her feet spread to either side of his own, fists once again on hips, hair swung aside with a sharp toss of her head, revealing bare shoulder, neck, face, and intense blue eyes. This wasn't the lioness, female or not, this was the lion—the greatest hunter of them all. The grandest alpha of the whole pack, no matter her gender.

"Holy crap, Melanie! Who the hell was that?"

"This," she brushed a hand down her length from neck to groin, "is the woman about to drag you back to her bed."

Josh staggered willingly to his feet to be led to his doom.

MELANIE WOKE ABRUPTLY in the dark. Alone. She knew it without having to roll over and look. An empty bed felt different. A shiver rolled up her spine; some dream, barely forgotten, but one that had racked up her heart rate and breathing.

An odd noise came from the living room. A soft sound she couldn't identify.

She donned a t-shirt and sweatpants and crept to the door. A single light lit the kitchen table.

Joshua. The dream retreated a little further.

He sat with an untouched glass of milk rested beside the small laptop. His bare back so beautiful in the softness of the indirect light. Once again he wore jeans that rode low enough to show he wore nothing else. His focus was absolute.

Melanie watched him type for a long time. He'd pause, stare off into the darkness, seeing something, searching in the shadows. Then he'd put his head back down, his fingers flashing across the keys once more before he even had time to look down at the screen.

She was in such trouble with this man. They had been here together days, merely days, yet it felt as normal as if it had been forever. At some point, she'd get a call and she'd be gone. New York, Paris, Milan, Tokyo. The only reason she wasn't gone already, other than the stupid swimsuit issue, was that she hadn't updated her website to show herself as available for bookings.

It wasn't rebound. Yes, Carlo had left her, but over the years she'd been single as much as she'd been with anyone, more. That wasn't the problem. The problem was Joshua Harper.

It was his doing that pieces of her shield lay unrecoverably shattered on the condo's floor. The protection she'd always kept so close about her heart didn't keep out Joshua. Or the rest of *The Fabulous Five*. What did they now see and know that she'd never shown to anyone in her life?

Her anchors were gone.

Perhaps he was right. He wasn't good for her. Not safe. She shouldn't have pushed. After five years of marriage it was too soon for him. He'd latched onto her like a breath of fresh air, but that was all. And she'd latched onto him as a fantasy of...

She couldn't quite make up an excuse for herself, but it was there. Wasn't it? Domesticity? Of belonging, if only for a moment of time?

Joshua would get lost in some novel, or settle somewhere,

put down roots, and never want to leave. He struck her as a complete homebody.

Then she'd be royally screwed.

What if she could adapt? Settle in...Seattle? The runways were New York, Milan, Paris. The photo shoots were mostly New York. Seattle connected to nothing in her life.

Better to just end it, be done with it, and get the hell back to New York where no one knew her. Declare it as one night of marvelous sex and cash it in while she was still ahead before—

"Hey, you. Didn't see you there. I tried not to wake you."

Joshua stood a single step in front of her. His chest all shadows; safe to hide in. But Melanie had never liked hiding from her problems. She'd done it—when the dark clouds of pending depression had threatened to stomp her ass—she'd done it. But she didn't want to hide from this problem.

"Melanie?"

Or did she? "Sorry to interrupt your writing. I'll just go back to bed."

"No, wait. I'm done anyway. I just had to get something down. You inspire me, pretty one."

"Pretty one? *Pretty one!* Is that what I am?" Fuck! That's what her mother always called her right before she struck. When Melanie was a powerless little girl. Well she wasn't powerless any—

"Whoa! Whoa! Whoa!" Josh held up both hands.

If he'd stepped forward, she might have struck out at him. Pay back all that pain, all that fear that—

"Melanie."

"What!"

"Take a breath."

"What?"

"Take a deep breath."

"Look, I'm breathing just fine." She waved to her chest. That's all men saw of her anyway.

"You're on the verge of hyperventilating."

"If I do, it's my own damn problem!" Then she heard her own voice; heard the shrillness that sounded so like her mother's. How had it spun in on her? And tonight of all nights? She and Joshua made such love and here she was... She could feel her cheeks flash hot as she bolted for the bedroom.

She didn't make it. Josh stopped her easily; his casual, unthinking strength a comfort rather than a cause of fear. He led her away from the safety of the bedroom, from the safety of the bathroom where she could lock the door, the shower where she could weep and no one would hear. He guided her to the couch. Sat her down. Wrapped a throw around her shoulders. Then he fetched his untouched milk.

"Sip this. Slowly."

When she didn't unclench her fists from inside the blanket where they were bunched close below her neck, he held the glass to her lips. She was forced to take a swallow or have it dribbling down her chin.

It was warm, soothing.

She could feel it moving down, into her belly. Her breathing slowed, damn him. And her heart rate along with it.

Finally, she simply leaned her head into the middle of his chest. He set down the glass of milk and wrapped his arms around her blanketed shoulders. She was unable to speak past her own embarrassment. Now was when he left her. Now was when he decided she wasn't worth the trouble. In the past... Actually, no one had been allowed to see this in the past. No one had ever seen The Great Melanie at her most fallible.

"Well..."

Here it came.

"You did mention being less than perfect, didn't you?" His voice was light, amused.

She had.

"I'm still not seeing it."

Melanie jerked upright to protest. But in the motion, she clipped his chin with the back of her head.

Hard!

His curses and intermittent, "Ow! Ow! Ow! My tong-ga!" would have been funny. Was funny. God she was such a mess that she started to laugh. Beyond funny, it was ridiculous.

The laugh swept her. They were two such ludicrous people.

She wiped at her eyes to see Joshua's expression shift slowly from pain to amusement to laughing himself.

"Ow! Ow! Don' make me laugh! Hurth!"

That tipped her right off the deep end. She collapsed into his lap, right onto... Well, wasn't that interesting. No questioning her effect on Joshua's body, not even when he was in pain.

His bare belly was right there. She put her lips against it and blew a loud raspberry.

His laugh turned into a high and silly giggle, intermixed with "Ow! Ow! Ow!" Gods he was so cute.

She blew another raspberry against his ticklish spot.

He twitched. Pushed at her.

She managed one more before he leveraged her away.

The next moment his mouth was on hers and if his tongue was still hurting, he showed no signs of it.

He swept her up in his arms, blanket and all, and carried her back to bed without once breaking the kiss.

CHAPTER 11

"*W*here does it come from, Melanie?"

They'd woken together, sometime well into the morning. Rather than simply expecting sex first thing, Joshua merely held her. Again, they had slept wrapped around each other.

She discovered that she was past keeping secrets from Joshua. Past being coy, or pretending to be. When had that happened?

"What are your parents like?" she had to know his frame of reference.

"They're all right. Retired a couple years ago to Florida. How stereotypical New York can you get? I try to see them a few times a year, whenever I'm, I was, in the area to review a restaurant. We're good. Not close, but good. Why?"

She held onto him hard, hoping against hope that he'd still be there when she was done telling him about hers. No one on the planet knew anything at all about her parents other than Russell, who knew only the tiniest sliver, and Perrin. And even she didn't know the details. Melanie would bet that was one story that hadn't traveled to Jo and Cassidy. There were some things they wouldn't understand. Of the three of them, only Perrin had also known such fear.

"I don't know how to tell this," she rolled her face into his chest looking for strength and, oddly, found it.

"Just say it. I'll still be here when you're done."

Some little girl part of her wanted him to promise. Maybe he already had. In Joshua's arms was the safest place she'd ever been. *Just do it, Melanie.* She took a deep breath and began.

"When I was eleven, I woke up to hear a terrible fight going on outside my bedroom. Apparently my father had decided I was pretty enough for him to spend some time with."

Joshua's body went rigid. His voice, at least an octave lower, ground out, "Did he touch you?" It was the first time she'd ever heard anger in his voice and it would have been terrifying if it was aimed at her. He'd shifted in a heartbeat from thoughtful lover to powerful bull-male. The kind you didn't want to upset.

"He never had the chance. Mom caught him halfway through my bedroom door on his first foray. In minutes, we were in the car and gone. I had clothes and schoolbooks, not much else. We never went back."

"Three cheers for her."

"No," she tried to sit up to judge his face, but he was holding her so tightly she couldn't move even that much. "You don't understand. She was yelling at him about the risk of damaging me. My first big photo shoot was scheduled for the next morning."

"At eleven?"

"I started out as a hand model," she held up one before her eyes as if she could see what was so special about them, but had never spotted it. "In the first years I made over thirty percent of my income from my hands. I still accept a dozen or so hand shoots a year. Sometimes for the oddest thing. Jewelry sure, but also holding a Coke can, a fine ink pen... No soap commercials. Risk of rash."

"How did the shoot go?"

"The photographer's cat scratched me and they had to get another model. My mother slapped me so hard we had to cancel two face shoots as well because my face was swollen. I missed a week of school because you could still see the palm print on my cheek. Those first months living in the car together were hard."

"You—" His voice choked off. His anger beyond speech.

"Mom ran my career with an iron fist for seven years, though she never struck me again anywhere that would show. By the time I was eighteen, I was a lot smarter. She'd been waiting for that moment, had been focusing all her efforts towards the big payouts. She had *Playboy, Hustler,* and a couple of porn movie companies all lined up for the day I became legal."

Joshua merely ground his teeth.

Usually when she'd thought of those years she felt ill, misused, and so very alone. But now she simply felt disconnected. She could have been reading a school report aloud for all she felt. Again, the safety of Joshua's arms.

"Did you—" There was no doubt as to his feeling on this. He wasn't some man asking if there were salacious photos he had missed somewhere. This was a man angry almost past tolerance.

"No. Never. If you see a naked photo of me, it's a fake. Not even a peep shot from the changing areas backstage at a runway. I gained a rather fierce reputation by smashing high-end camera equipment pretty early on."

"Well done you!"

"I did a family divorce, got custody of myself, so to speak. Put out a restraining order against my mother. Shed myself of her name, that is why I use no last name. I let her keep the money she'd embezzled as my manager."

"You let her keep—"

"I didn't want it. Not after her slimy hands had been all over it. Actually, every account I was a signatory on, I signed over to charity. I'm sure she had accounts I didn't know about, but I bet I got most of it. The day I turned eighteen I was broke, but I was my own woman. And I was in demand. I'd studied business like hell and have been my own manager since that day. I own a small studio apartment free and clear in a secure building in Manhattan. Everything else—everything, went into savings." She smiled and kissed Joshua's chest. He still hadn't let her up and it felt wonderful. "I'm very well off."

"Shit!"

"What?"

"I was wrong before." She tried to read his voice, but she couldn't. The anger was gone but she couldn't tell what had replaced it.

"Wrong about what?"

"About the whole perfect thing."

"Blew my cover, did I?" She tried to smile as she said it. She really hoped this wasn't where he pushed her away. And she should never have mentioned all the money. Bad slip.

He finally released her. Rolled slightly until they lay face to face, just inches apart. His dark eyes were intent, warm, welcoming. No signs of disgust or avarice. Every time she second-guessed his motivations, she'd been wrong.

"Totally blew your cover," Joshua acknowledged with a brush of knuckles along her cheek. "What's the word for someone who's better than perfect?"

She shoved against his shoulder which barely moved him. He was far stronger than he looked.

He leaned in and kissed her.

She let herself melt into the kiss.

"Wait," he murmured against her lips. "What's better than that?"

Then he showed her just what he really thought of her.

CHAPTER 12

For a whole week Melanie let herself play house. During the days she worked with Perrin on her business plan and consulted with Tamara after school on her new line.

In the evenings she and Joshua began exploring the local restaurants from the old tradition of The Merchant Café to the little Pho noodle shop on the corner. At night she had the best lover imaginable.

And they never shut up around each other. Joshua's characters were starting to take shape. He was cast building and between them they worked out how his characters walked and talked, their backgrounds and how they reacted to different stresses. Teaching Joshua how to do the walks enough to feel them with his body had left them both in tears with laughter.

Joshua held Melanie's hand when they took long strolls along the Seattle waterfront. They would walk an hour or more because they were so enjoying the discussions.

Kate was now one of his main characters.

"She walks just like you did that night," Joshua's eyes went dreamy at the memory.

She had more where that came from.

"Though I gave her thick dark hair. She's a chef who runs a television network."

"Who lives where?"

"How should I know? That weird top suite of the Chrysler building?" he'd tossed it out flippantly.

Melanie's spontaneous laugh had apparently settled that idea for Joshua. So, they'd gone about the task of designing her multi-story condo. It was all a great game.

During the day while she was at Perrin's, he'd be at Angelo's or the Pioneer Square condo pounding out words. In the evening she'd read through them, marking the bits she liked and the bits she didn't. He had a turn of phrase that made her smile when she least expected it.

One afternoon she'd received a text to meet him at the urban park on the high side of Second and Madison. She found him sitting on a bench in the bricked yard, shaded by leafed-out maple trees. Melanie could easily spend the day just watching him work.

But the sixth sense Joshua had developed about her presence had him turning within moments though she'd come up behind him. The afternoon traffic was loud, the metro buses shuffling and roaring.

"How?"

"Me and Superman."

A quick scan and she spotted the tall coffee shop window in which they were both clearly reflected. "No, Joshua. Just you. Superman didn't have eyes in the back of his head."

JOSH LOVED that Melanie had both spotted his cheat and let him have the win anyway. He kept his kiss brief because they were in a public place and he didn't want some random scandal photographer to get a photo and make her life miserable.

"C'mon. I just discovered this place that I've got to show you." He offered his arm.

She slipped in her hand and he led her two blocks up the hill and toward a building that filled an entire city block, six or seven stories of diamond-shaped glass. He waited until she spotted the sign.

"The Public Library." He could hear the blasé tone. Nothing was as good as NYPL; the New York Public Library was one of the best libraries on the planet after all.

"Trust me," Joshua was grinning as he led her inside.

"Stacks. So what's the big deal?" The place was bustling, but it was just stacks on the first floor.

Without a word, he led her up the escalator. And the world opened above them. Computers and comfortable meeting rooms ranged far and wide across the floor. Light poured in from above. The modern version of the NYPL's Rose Main Reading Room, with lines of reading desks and fifty-foot ceiling muraled like the sky.

"It's pretty."

Rather than speaking, he led her to an elevator and took them to the top floor. The view from the top was nice, but nothing spectacular. Without comment he led her down the ramp that circled downward. Level bookshelves ranged off to either side, but the aisle descended in a spiral row by row.

They were in the 100s before she noticed the numbers painted on the floors, the walls, the bookcases. By the 200s she was looking a little dazzled as they completed the first lap of their descent.

"How many stories?" she barely whispered.

"Four full laps to go from 000s to 900s. This isn't New York. You can just walk into the stacks without a catalog query and a request to a librarian. Any subject. Look!"

He led her into 391 and there was costume and history. Just as he'd hoped she got all gooey-eyed. She reached out to touch some of them like old friends.

"I'd show you 746, but I'll never see you again if I do."

She leaned and began whispering in French close by his ear. It took him time to translate, especially as he didn't know some of the words and he had to kind of cobble together the sense of them. Then he caught on.

The gorgeous lover of his was describing things that maybe even the *Kama Sutra* didn't know about. Things she'd do tonight if he led her to that section directly.

He considered blushing, considered it seriously as they were standing in the middle of the library stacks. Instead he took a deep breath.

"You are not motivating me to do anything but drag you back to the condo right away."

"Then you get *zéro. Rien. Nada. Zilch. Nichts. Ny—*"

"I get the idea. I get the idea. Why do you know how to say 'no' in so many languages."

"It is, how you say, useful around men."

"You're killing me with the accent." One of the things she'd started doing was that all of their sex was done in French. It was definitely improving his language skills, but it also made him horny as hell every time she said even a word or two in the language.

And she bloody well knew it. *Merde!* But the woman was going to be the death of him yet.

He zigzagged her through staircases that cut across the middle of the loops instead of walking the descending spiral of the full catalog.

Joshua let her walk into 746 on her own. Textile Arts and near the very end of the category, one of the most impressive fashion collections he'd ever seen.

MELANIE RANGED ALONG THE BOOKCASES. There were references here she hadn't known existed. Other volumes she'd only seen in Óscar de la Renta's personal collection.

But the greatest surprise was that Joshua had found this for her. He'd had clearly scouted out the two non-fiction sections she'd most care about and given them to her as a treat.

He stood in the "bead embroidery" section pretending interest so that she wouldn't feel rushed. What was he doing to her? How had she come to care so much about the man?

Melanie didn't fall for men; she *chose* lovers. Carefully, with forethought and discernment. Joshua simply swept her feet from beneath her.

This week held other surprises. Apparently, having been beaten back twice in the same week by Joshua, her depression had given up its attacks and fled. At least for now. Melanie didn't even feel it lurking, though it couldn't be completely gone. That was too much to ask.

It was often six months or once whole a year between attacks that drove her to go to ground for a week. She'd always managed to hold it off when there was work scheduled, but this time it had been driven away by the man now browsing through the fabric dyeing section. Future retribution worried her some-what, but she did her best not to contemplate the problem.

She and this man had bared their hearts to one another. They'd spoken of their pasts, the cracks in his marriage—only visible in hindsight. Her failure with Russell. The revelation of her childhood had taken down the last of the walls between them.

The one thing they carefully didn't discuss was the future. They curled up each night as if it might be their last together, and woke with a shared look of surprise and wonder.

This was as close as they'd come, his showing her something

he knew she would love, this beautiful fashion collection just begging to be studied and enjoyed over time. She wondered if he was conscious of it, that he was trying to find reasons for her to stay in Seattle even if there was no possible way for it to work without destroying her career.

It was an eloquent statement and she would gladly repay him for the effort by delivering every single thing she had whispered into his ear.

But they both knew it was impossible.

About that there could never be any words.

*a*ngelo's two restaurants were open over the weekend and closed Mondays and Tuesdays, so everyone had shifted their schedules to match. Jo managed the Pike Place Market on that schedule. Russell and Cassidy were freelancers so they were always busy, but were more likely to take time off on Monday and Tuesday.

Perrin was caught in between, with the kids in school and her husband as the stage manager for Emerald City Opera. So, she worked Monday through Friday, but the shop ran Wednesday through Sunday.

When Melanie arrived on Monday morning, the front door on Second Avenue was locked. But she spotted the light in the back of the darkened shop. She went around to the alley door, picking her way around a couple of city-ugly dumpsters to tap on the back door, though the alley itself was open and totally harmless.

Perrin let her in. No seamstresses today, so apparently they too were working the Wednesday through Sunday schedule. The shop was quiet and peaceful, but Perrin was still a whorl of activity with a half dozen projects spread about.

"Tomorrow is Tuesday, you know," Perrin stated as if that explained something.

"Which means what?"

"It means that you and Josh are coming to dinner. We all go to Maria and Hogan's every Tuesday."

Melanie blinked. It was no longer a shock that she was included, just a pleasant surprise. "What do we bring?"

"Oh, first timers just show up."

She reminded herself to talk to Joshua. Melanie didn't like the idea of being a "first timer," of being somehow different from the others. They'd think up something appropriate. Or he would. Her culinary skills were mostly limited to reheating the wonders Joshua prepared for her.

"They're also probably going sailing tomorrow."

"That is so not going to happen," sailing was not a Melanie sport. Not even a little. She recalled touring Russell's boat on that wonderful-horrible Valentine's Day that had been the end of their relationship as lovers. She felt slightly nauseous just remembering the oily swirl of water across the bilge exposed through the missing floorboard.

Perrin laughed, "Yeah, our first trip didn't work out so well either." By Perrin's grimace it must have been something spectacular. "I almost lost Bill and we both almost lost Jaspar. The boys still go out with Russell, but Tamara and I almost never go with."

They chatted a while, talked business for a bit. But something was bothering Perrin. She was holding back, which wasn't like her. Neither was she working on a design or a construction while she talked.

Melanie tried teasing it out of her without success, so finally she just asked.

"Well, you've been so kind to me, I hate to ask. But Russell said I should."

"Perrin, spill it or I'll force you to make me a dress out of that very expensive fabric you had the other day."

Perrin's eyes slid aside for a moment, but her smile increased rather than diminishing. "Not yet," but declined to explain that comment even when Melanie pushed.

"The thing is," Perrin went to a clothing rack in the corner and fussed with a line of garment bags. "I answered the phone yesterday. I really shouldn't do that, but Raquel was busy with a customer and I happened to be in the shop with Tammy and... Well, I..."

Melanie waited her out until Perrin spilled it all forth in a single breath. "It was *Fashion Alive* magazine. Not that editor I told you about, the ad department. They had a last-minute cancellation—after they were already in layout—so they have to fill the ad space. The editor told them, I have no idea why, that I could fill it on short notice. She even personally guaranteed that it would be exceptional, as if. They're giving it to me gratis if I can send the images by tomorrow."

"Are you kidding, Perrin? That's spectacular! They're on the verge of challenging *Marie Claire*. A third-page ad is over fifty thousand dollars. Gratis is enormous."

Perrin's nerves were wilder than usual. She began folding and refolding a piece of lapis-blue corduroy that must be for one of Tamara's projects; the blue had pop, it was a thoughtful selection. Melanie grabbed Perrin's hands to still them and sat down on a stool. That forced Perrin to come to rest opposite her.

"It's a game changer, isn't it, Melanie? You told me one was coming, but it's too soon. I'm not ready."

"Yes," Melanie had to acknowledge, "stepping into *Fashion Alive* is a game changer. Even a small ad will have a real impact on your business. But this is really too important an opportunity to miss. It's a far better exposure than you could afford to buy for at least six months, probably a year."

"More like forever." Perrin groaned.

No matter how good she was, Perrin still didn't understand the scale of her talent. "Not forever, but you can worry about that later. Right now, you are far more ready than I thought you were at the beginning of the week. I'll commit to staying at least another week so that I can show you how to tweak the plan to make it work. You'll have to bring on more people. I already talked to the owner of the shop next door. He said he would love to rent the back room; it is empty right now. So you could make a door right there," Melanie pointed at the wall, "and create a large sewing room pretty easily."

"Okay, I kinda hoped you'd say that it made sense, but that isn't the favor I wanted to ask."

Melanie kept a tight hold on both of Perrin's hands as she could still feel Perrin's nerves humming.

"Would you be my model? I can't pay very much, but you'd be so perfect for these designs and it really freaks Cassidy and Jo when I make them pose and—"

Melanie cut her off. "Yes."

"Really?"

"No, I said that just to get you to calm down," Melanie laughed at the abrupt disappointment that flashed onto her friend's features. "Of course I will, Perrin. I love your designs. They always make me look so at the edge of new ideas. I'd be thrilled to pose for you."

"Wow! Uh, how much do you—"

"How about that dress I mentioned?"

Perrin's smile was electric. "Well, that might be cheating, but it's a deal." She didn't explain that enigmatic comment either.

"It's a deal!" Melanie and Perrin spoke in unison and together shook their still double-clasped hands up and down.

"Two other things I should probably mention."

"What are they?" Melanie was pleased. It would be fun to do a shoot, even a little one.

"First, Russell rented my old apartment upstairs as a studio and he said to call him as soon as I found you. I should have called you earlier. I was trying to get up the nerve when you came by. He wants to do it right away. Are you okay that it's him?"

Melanie took a deep breath and checked in with herself about modeling for Russell. She was feeling wonderful, much of which was Joshua's doing. And it *would* be great to work with Russell again. He always found a way to make her look so alluring. Even if it was just a third-page ad, the discards would create some fresh material for her website.

"Call him now."

Perrin squeezed her hands hard.

"What's the other thing?"

Perrin reached for the phone and began dialing. She kept her head down as she spoke.

Melanie could barely hear her mumble.

"The cancellation was a four-page spread in the front twenty."

MELANIE WAS STILL TRYING to digest that bit of news as she worked her way into the first dress and did her own makeup.

When Tamara arrived from school, she was instantly tasked with brushing out Melanie's hair. Not a single snarl or twist allowed. Her hair was always either a straight fall or in a ponytail. Her trademark hair was never up, never teased, and god forbid never colored. That was part of her contracts; it also vastly simplified styling choices for the designer. Which many complained about, but ultimately seemed to appreciate.

A four-page spread in the front twenty. The only thing that caused a cancellation like that was a revelation of illegal activity, like design theft. Even the buyout of a fashion house wouldn't cause that late a change. All of the space was prepaid and they were way past the payment and the late-cancellation deadlines, so the magazine would have no financial loss and could afford to give it away. She hadn't looked at their rates recently but, the last time she had, it was over a hundred and thirty thousand dollars—per page.

Melanie considered kicking out a text to some industry friends to find out who had choked and how. There were only a dozen or so advertisers who could afford that major a spread to begin with. The front twenty was the stomping grounds of only the best and the very well-funded who typically reserved that space over a year ahead. She'd text later.

"The editor was one of your customers," Melanie knew it was right the instant she said it.

Perrin shrugged in the mirror. "I don't work front of shop much anymore, so she mostly dealt with Raquel. But after she'd bought three pieces in a single fling, she insisted on meeting me. I only had a few minutes before Bill picked me up, but she was extremely excited. She looked great in one of my day dresses, very chic and flirty."

"That's an ardent fan, Perrin. They are rare and precious people who can make all of the difference." Thinking of fans, maybe she should call Joshua. She'd come to accept that he was a fan of her public image, even forcing him to unearth the *Teen Vogue* when he'd confessed to owning a copy. She'd looked good. Young, but good. She couldn't be angry because Joshua had also proved time and again how clearly he also saw the real Melanie.

"Look who I found just hanging around to carry my gear for me," Russell announced as he burst in the back door.

Joshua peeked at her over Russell's broad shoulders.

Russell winked at her from where he'd stopped, completely filling the back doorway with his broad-shouldered frame and two camera cases.

Joshua had to shove past the grinning man. He crossed the studio and reached for her.

"Don't touch the hair. Tamara's been working too hard for you to muss it up."

She could see the temptation cross his features.

"Don't even think it, Harper. Just don't."

Instead, he held her hand and kissed her on the lips very sweetly. She gave him a careful hug, then turned back to the mirror to check the damage. Well worth it.

THE SHOOT ITSELF WAS A BLUR, they always were. Melanie let herself become a vehicle for the photographer's instructions. She'd done photo shoots with Russell: before, during, and after they'd been lovers. It had made little difference; they were professionals doing the jobs they both did best.

But Joshua affected her, she could feel it. She'd walk toward the camera and recall the heat she'd seen fire up in Joshua's eyes when she'd worn only a t-shirt instead of one of the sexiest pant suits she'd ever seen.

She would turn to look over her shoulder at the camera and see Joshua standing behind Russell with a smile so wide she wanted to go and kiss it off his face.

They went through a dozen pieces, Perrin and Tamara scrambling back and forth between the downstairs design studio and the upstairs apartment-turned-photo studio. Russell had Joshua stand in to give her positioning for a pose—something about them being the same height was desirable, but Russell didn't stop to explain—and then move him carefully aside without jostling her. Even after he was gone, she could feel herself leaning on his shoulder and smiling from somewhere down inside.

For some reason that he'd never explained and she'd never

asked, Russell never used her face in his ads. He always hid it with hair, hat, shadow, or other composition. Not this shoot.

The time flew. At some point, they fed her. Later, Bill and Jaspar came to pick up Tamara and instead ended up being recruited by Russell to the dozens of odd jobs involved in a shoot: angling reflectors, holding meter cards, shifting umbrella lights, moving props without disturbing the model's position, flapping boards in front of a large fan to create little gusts, and a myriad of other tasks.

MELANIE AND JOSHUA were actually reentering the condo by the time she came back to herself, just like a couple returning from a good day's work. Both chattering away about how fun it had been as he unlocked and held doors for her to pass through first.

The afternoon had been an extravagant whirlwind of innovative clothes and immense fun. Joshua had taken to making the occasional funny face over Russell's shoulder, several causing Melanie to crack up and lose a pose.

"I *love* photo shoot modeling!"

Joshua laughed at her passion as she set her purse in its usual spot then did a twirl in the middle of the living room.

"It's the single thing I loved the most. More than the runway. It's that back and forth with a truly skilled photographer."

"Uh-huh."

The man was slouched against the wall with his arms folded across his chest. That sparkle in his eyes and grin on his face whenever he was just watching her. He never tired of it and she never felt self-conscious in front of him. She just felt...appreciated.

"It's like you were saying when you got that first scene written." She spun over and pinned him to the wall for a moment

167

with her lips and body. Even when she pulled back enough to continue, she used her body to keep him there. "That energy the character gave you and you gave her. It just hums inside you."

And it had been such a joy. None of them were being paid and none of them cared. They were all there to help a friend. Well, she'd get a killer dress out of it, because that was the only kind of dress Perrin made. She'd felt a little guilty about requesting such luxurious fabrics, but a free four-page spread would pay it back in the first day's orders.

"Joshua, we have to totally re-do Perrin's plan. An ad spread of any size wasn't supposed to happen until next year."

"You also didn't factor in having the most beautiful woman on the planet being the signature model."

She giggled at the compliment. Melanie never giggled, but she couldn't help herself. Joshua simply made her feel that special.

"Let's go dancing!"

And that's exactly what they did. They hit Pioneer Square.

"Hey look!" Joshua pointed at the sign above a bar right in the heart of the Square.

"The J&M Café. Oldest bar in Seattle." Melanie read in wonder. "The J&M Mutual Admiration Society now has a base of operations."

They drank one beer each, laughed like they'd had a dozen, and rocked out to the live band right up to the two-a.m. closing time.

CHAPTER 14

*R*ussell called them to come early to Maria's Tuesday night dinner. Cassidy and Russell lived a few blocks north of the Market in Belltown. Maria and Hogan lived in a building that looked directly down on the cobbled streets, booths, and the waterfront. The apartment was cozy for a couple rather than spacious and begging for expansion like the Pioneer Square condo.

They'd decorated it with a tasteful eye and an old-world elegance that fit them. Kitchen, bedroom, and office all opened off one wall. The living room boasted a large brown leather sofa facing the view and several comfortable-looking armchairs to either side. Bookcases down the left wall. The back of the living room was the domain of a massive oak table that could easily seat a dozen.

Josh hadn't been sure what to bring. Just a bottle of wine seemed lame. And going up against a patissier of Maria's skill also kept desserts off the list of possible things to bring. He'd settled on a platter of build-it-yourself bruschetta. He premade and toasted the thin rounds of French baguette and rubbed them all lightly with garlic. Then he'd made a large plate with a pile of fresh-made mozzarella cheese at the center and surrounded it with mounds of slivered olives, chiffonaded basil, diced sun-dried tomatoes, and a half-dozen other toppings.

It earned him a hug from Maria and earned Russell a swat from her when he'd tried to grab a fistful of the toasts to munch on. So, Joshua would count that as a two-fold success.

"You know," Russell absently flexed his sore knuckles as he turned to Melanie, "I won't use any image without your approval. But I think you'll like these. I really hope so because I didn't have time to make any other variations. I already ran them by Perrin and she's over the moon." He rubbed his mouth where Josh would bet Perrin had planted a smacking kiss of thanks.

"But no pressure to like them," Melanie laughed that beautiful laugh of hers then tugged Josh along to go look at them. The four prints were laid down on the bright oak of the big dining room table.

Josh had never really looked at Russell's work, except the landscapes on the walls of Angelo's restaurants. Those evoked a specific, soothing emotion making it a comfortable place to dine rather than merely eat. But these fashion photographs were something else again. Even to his untrained eye each was a straight-shot punch to the gut.

Melanie was posing—with herself! That's why he'd had to stand in to help her find the right poses. Rather than four images of her, there were a total of nine on the four pages. In the first, the pantsuit clad Melanie was resting a casual hand on a friend's shoulder, except the friend was also Melanie, dressed for a night on the town and laughing at a joke just told.

In the next, she leaned against her own back, clad once in a dynamo black power suit of jacket and skinny spring-green dress, the other in the slacks, blouse, and loosened tie of waterfall silk of a woman supremely competent and confident—

enough so to not need the power suit. Each appeared to be scoffing at the other's presumption.

Sportswear was clearly the subject of a grudge match between two ponytailed Melanies somehow glaring at each other but also, just as clearly, giving the camera a nudge-and-a-wink look that made him want to laugh.

The last page. He wanted a life-size poster of that last image. Melanie three ways. Three brilliant evening gowns the color of new leaves—each radiating sex in its own way. But it wasn't just sex, it was the raw power of the incredibly feminine form within. The first with deep cleavage and soft flowing folds, the second with a form-hugging sleekness, and the last dress so thoroughly covering her body that it was impossible to avoid imagining the woman beneath.

Separately they were beautiful, together they were astonishing.

Across all nine poses, Josh could pick out each woman. Could see the powerful, the shy, the playful, and all of the others Melanie had told him about and walked for him. But there was something more, if he could only identify it.

Melanie gave Russell hands-down approval. They went to the computer in Hogan's small home office to sign the model releases and send them off to the magazine.

Josh stayed to study the pictures and see if he could figure out what he wasn't seeing.

"She loves you so very much."

He startled to see that Maria had come up beside him to look down at the images of Melanie. Then Maria's words registered. "She what?"

"Look," she nodded down to the nine figures looking back at him. "If you can't see it in how she looks at you, it is right there in all of the pictures. Russell is very skilled, but even he couldn't have done that if it weren't in her to give."

And now Josh could see it. He could see that all nine of the women before him were also the final woman. It was a woman Melanie hadn't shown him before. It wasn't the lioness who had devoured his heart. It was the beautiful woman who had offered him her own.

She reentered the room from the office door not ten feet away, laughing about something with Russell. Then she turned to him and her face shifted. It was subtle. If he hadn't been studying the images before him, if Maria hadn't pointed out the common thread, he wouldn't have understood the change.

There was no question, Maria was right.

Melanie loved him.

Just maybe she loved him as much as he now understood he loved her.

"WHAT IS IT?" Melanie had asked Joshua three times during dinner, but he had only shaken his head and looked away. Something had shifted after he'd seen those wonderful ads Russell had made.

He took another bite of his Italian cheesecake, clearly to avoid answering her question.

"You begin to scare me, Joshua." She kept her voice low. She really hoped he wasn't somehow seeing her again as the super-model. He was the only one who truly saw past the external beauty—past the make-believe she presented to the world—far past the view she couldn't block from Russell. At first it had scared her, but she had come to cherish that about him.

Russell had indeed made her look fabulous. These ads were going to, as Perrin would say, kick ass. But if they'd made Joshua lose that unique perspective he had of her, it wouldn't have been worth it.

Maria and Hogan had propped up the first three images for display along one of the bookcases and tacked the fourth on the wall which was covered with candid shots, mostly of the people in this room. The photo shoot was definitely the news of the evening and the images were a near constant topic.

Only now did it strike her that Maria might intend to add that image permanently to the collection—the extended family collection. As if she belonged. And looking at the others she did. It was impossible. She knew that family, in any form, was a deception. Except not in the extended family that centered around Maria and her three chosen daughters.

Melanie set the idea aside very gently. She knew it was precious and she didn't want to break it.

To keep Russell's ego in check after all of the compliments on the shoot, Perrin and Tammy had started a campaign of teasing him horribly about anything they could come up with. Cassidy had joined in on the side of her husband and Jo was refereeing in such a way as to make it more lively. Cassidy had been right; Jo was sneaky.

As the sun set beyond the Olympics, candlelight replaced sunlight. The room was crowded and loud, filled with the sounds of friends simply glad to be together.

And no one was treating her strangely at all. Not because of the photos, not because she was a supermodel. No one...except Joshua.

Maria and Hogan sat at either end of the main table, but with the restaurant staff and other friends, there were sufficient numbers that they spilled over into the living area, returning to the table only to restock plates from the vast trays of food that had been prepared and to add a tease to the merry battle surrounding Russell. It was cheerful mayhem.

She became aware that Joshua was studying her closely. The noise around the table was sufficient to create something of a bubble around them.

"You," Joshua whispered softly enough that only she would hear it, "are the one who is scaring me."

He must have seen her confusion.

His answer was to lean in and give her a kiss that reassured her more than any words could have done. It was a kiss flavored of ricotta, chocolate, and strawberries—Maria's Italian cheesecake. It lingered, tested, and asked. She didn't know the question, but she answered and felt the shift inside her as she did so.

Her heart didn't pound, instead it beat as smooth and silkily as the texture of the dessert. Joshua's kiss was a place she could go to be lost forever. Time, sound, the external world stopped. Nothing existed but them, their connection, their being together in this lingering moment.

When the kiss ended, her ears were buzzing.

And that was the only sound in the room.

From one end of the table to the other, everyone was looking at them. Even those sitting in the living room chairs and sofa were silent. Cassidy and Perrin actually had tears in their eyes. Jo had rested her head on Angelo's broad shoulder.

Tammy broke the silence with a thirteen-year old's sigh that sent a ripple of laughter around the room. Then Jaspar offered a ten-year-old boy's view with a loud, "Eww!" which shifted the sound of the laughter yet again and slowly rekindled conversations.

Melanie didn't blush when she was kissed. More than one of her clinches had ended up on the cover of *People* and a fair number had graced the cover of the *National Enquirer*. But now the heat roared to her face.

She considered facing the laughter in defiance. But it was a friendly sound that made her feel both welcome and fortunate. So, rather than pulling on her imperious cloak, she did as Joshua did and turned her full attention to her dessert—only too aware of how closely their legs pressed together beneath the table.

CHAPTER 15

osh had wanted to help, but over the next week Melanie only let him do so when she was stuck on some particular aspect of Perrin's business strategy.

"Your job, Joshua, is to write. You wrote those two press releases for her, which were wonderful, thank you. But that is not your passion. You have quit your job to write a novel. Go, write your novel."

As if he could just wave a wand and the typed pages would appear. So, he'd gone alone to his usual table at Angelo's and sat down to write.

He tried waving a fork of the boar-sausage pasta that Graziella had served him for lunch, but all it did was waft the delicious smell of garlic, sausages, and fresh basil; no novel magically appeared on the table or under it. He checked.

So he ate the pasta, ignored the gentle conversations of the late lunch crowd, and, as he'd done all week, turned back to his computer. He had his fictional world built. It was a crazy one that was nothing like he'd imagined.

He'd thought it might be a cozy murder mystery, a poisoning, half the people in the house guilty, the other half wishing they'd thought to kill the victim themselves, no one knowing who to trust. Not just cliché; way overdone cliché.

Melanie had pointed that out and he'd thrown away almost five thousand words.

Hard-boiled had been another dead lead. The Sam Spade of the culinary world, still referring to women as "dames" and guns as "heaters" though he lived in the modern world. It simply hadn't come together. That had only cost him a thousand words or so.

He'd tried to force it to be a police procedural: *CSI* does Pike Place Market. So not. Another thousand.

But this? He didn't know where it had come from. It was as much political thriller as anything else.

It had Kate his cooking channel executive, her useless playboy brother, Rika the criminal superhacker and part time sushi chef, and a silent Marine Force Recon turned butcher as her security. The cast reminded him of last night's second dinner at Maria's, just as diverse and off-the-wall fun as the first.

Melanie's triptych, now framed, had still hypnotized him and he still hadn't found a way to talk about his revelation. In love, both of them, and neither daring to say it aloud.

That's all his novel's plot needed to make it a complete train wreck—a love story.

Josh stopped with another forkful of pasta halfway to his mouth and stared at his screen.

He'd built his world: a tableau of people rife with quirks and shortcomings. He had a cool opening murder, there were so many interesting ways to kill off a chef.

But what if it wasn't a mystery? That's how these people fit together! It wasn't a foodie mystery; it was a foodie thriller.

And a love story.

He couldn't think the words without thinking of Melanie. All week, they still hadn't spoken a single word of the future.

Telling her that he loved her could ruin that. With love went commitment. Not just committing to relationship, but the mere act of loving meant connection.

And that had worked out so spectacularly badly for each of them. With their track record they shouldn't even start. There was a thought that hurt like hell.

Rather than speaking—rather than forcing a conversation neither of them had wanted to have—they lived the future one day at a time. They went for walks, made dinner plans, lunched with friends, and worked hard. Perrin's business was consuming Melanie's days and the novel his, but the nights were their own.

They bought little things for the Pioneer Square condo. Not for themselves but for the condo, because anything more might imply some form of permanence. A poster that would look good there. Bright pillows that cheered up the sofa. A couple of yoga exercise mats that Melanie was using to prove to Joshua just how inflexible he was. "I should teach a class called, 'Yoga for men who don't bend'!" She should, he for one would gladly pay to watch how she could move.

They were living a love story, one day at a time by continuing to pretend that tomorrow didn't exist.

His novel needed a love story. Not only wasn't his book a murder mystery, it wasn't a foodie thriller either. No. It was a foodie romantic suspense? It was crazy; that same kind of craziness that somehow made sense. Like him being in love with a supermodel who loved him back—ridiculous from the outside, wonderful from the inside.

The love story would be the main character, but would happen around and because of her. Would the woman be a restauranteur...no, too stereotypical. She'd be a competitor on Kate's show. No, still too normal. That had to be the victim. Maybe it was a thriller. What about a one-book love interest for Kate? A glorious affair rather than a happy ever after.

Another judge? One who…

Josh startled to realize that Melanie was sitting quietly on the other side of the table. They had brainstormed so much, that he didn't think about it, he just leapt in.

"I need another character. Interesting guy. Cooks a lot. Professional chef or the potential to be one. Not sure yet. He needs to be someone for my heroine to fall in love with."

"You."

He opened his mouth, then closed it.

Melanie took a deep breath and let it out slowly. Then her smile shone to life. "Wow! That was a surprise."

"I'm noticing that."

"Well," Melanie reached over to take a forkful of his pasta. "Oh that's so *délectable.* Angelo is definitely a food criminal because this is sinfully wonderful."

Then she looked at him more seriously.

"Any woman with the least common sense would fall in love with you, Joshua Harper."

He tried to catch his breath, but it was sticking somewhere in his chest. "You always struck me as a woman with immense common sense." How lame was that? He was begging.

"Thank you," she reached over to take another forkful. She made him wait while she ate another bite, her eyes remaining locked on his.

She took her time chewing, swallowing, reaching to take a sip of his iced tea.

He remained mute.

"Yes, I'm not sure that it is sensible, but I have fallen quite in love with you, Joshua. I find that it complicates things quite badly."

"I've *been* noticing that myself for over a week." There. He'd as good as said it. But it wasn't enough and he knew it. "I don't know if it was at our first meeting a couple months ago or the moment you threatened to Taser my ass, but I have discovered I am so very much in love with you. I'm sure this isn't just rebound. It's too big and too wonderful to be just... What?"

Melanie's smile had grown huge.

"What?"

"You are a man of many words."

He looked down at his computer screen, and then back up at her to make his point. He was.

"So, my man of words, what are you thinking?"

"I'm thinking I can write anywhere I have a laptop." He said the next part because it was true. "And you. I need you like I need to breathe. You inspire me. You make me want to be better —" He clamped his jaw shut. He was doing it again. Too many words.

Melanie tipped her head, her long hair making a blonde waterfall over her shoulder. "You are more romantic than I am, Joshua. But you are right. I have never looked as I did in those photos. I have spent the week since puzzling over that difference. I finally found it. During that entire photo shoot, I was thinking of you. I was thinking of the joy you bring me."

"So, what do we do?" Josh was sorry the second he asked, for the smile slid off Melanie's face. She bowed her head and her hair shuttered part of her face from him.

"This I don't know."

So, it was up to him. "Okay. Here's what we're going to do." His voice seemed confident, declaring that he had the answers, even if he didn't. Yet.

She looked up at him in uncertain hope.

"First, we will continue as we have been."

"Playing house as if we are a couple?" there was an edge to her voice.

"Making the most of each day because we choose to be together."

She brightened at that interpretation and nodded.

"Second, we start talking about what tomorrow may be. Not

what are we committing to. Let's make it…ah!" There was the metaphor he wanted.

He hit Save, then closed his laptop, shoving it and the now empty pasta bowl aside.

He nudged his iced tea closer to the middle of the table in case she wanted some more. "So, what are we really good at together?"

"Making love." She said it matter-of-factly but it sent the air whooshing out of his lungs. He continued when he managed to restart his breathing.

"Okay. I'd say better than 'really good' but I'll accept that. No, I was thinking that we're really exceptional at ideas. At coming up with ideas *and* making them happen. Do you know how rare that is? People have a thousand ideas, but never seem to get around to them. Those people make me crazy."

"Me too. Okay, so we make up ideas and do them. I still do not understand where you are going, Joshua." She ran a manicured finger down the side of the sweating tea glass as if trying to draw their completed path. That would be a good trick, as he only saw only a little of it himself.

He tapped his laptop. "We need to make up our own story, our own novel. We've already got the first meeting."

"Me trying to Taser you."

"Technically the second meeting, but thanks again for not pulling the trigger."

"It's a button."

"Whatever, thanks."

"*De rein.*"

"And we've both just admitted that we're quite completely gone on each other."

"You can say 'in love,' Joshua," her smile mocked him.

"I can. But I don't want to scare you."

"I'm already scared enough for it not to make much difference."

"Okay. I don't want to scare *me*, because being in love with a woman who is beyond perfect, which I still haven't found a word for, is definitely an unnerving experience. I keep waiting for you to snap out of it and look at me with utter disdain."

She reached out to brush the moisture-cool finger along his cheek. He took the opportunity to capture her hand and leave a kiss in the center of her palm. He loved watching her response to him as her lids half lowered and a sigh rippled through her.

Graziella passed by their table, "Get a room, you two." She dropped off a second iced tea and a spare napkin, leaving a smile in her wake. Gone too fast for Josh to even say thank you.

He turned back to Melanie, "My idea is, before you distract me any further. Let's brainstorm it out. We can't build a relationship any more easily than a runway show or a novel. We've got a great basis: we love each other, and we both want to find a way to make this work."

"We're supposed to write our own romance?"

"Yes. With its own happy ever after." He shrugged, "You have any better ideas, I'm open to them."

She studied him for a long moment in silence. He could see the brilliance that she hid so carefully from most others. It clicked away behind her eyes like a fine-tuned mechanism. The businesswoman analyzing the idea slowly gave way to the sensual lover who made his head spin.

"I think you are right."

"I am?" Shocked him—about a Taser's worth.

"Yes, we are both too smart to not find a way to make this work. But there is one thing that you must first do, Joshua."

"Name it."

"You must, without any extra words, tell me that you love me."

He almost started with "You make such difficult requests," but caught himself in time.

He still held her held her hand, so he rubbed a thumb over

the kiss on her palm as if making sure it stuck there. He looked into the most amazing blue eyes he'd ever seen. He let the brightness—that shone on him from the most unlikely of women—wash over him.

"I love you."

Her own response was equally simple and he knew his life had just been changed forever.

Graziella's quiet "Hallelujah" in the background he simply ignored.

CHAPTER 16

ashion Alive landed on the racks eight days later and the response was instantaneous and overwhelming.

At Melanie's advice, that evening they all retreated to Bill and Perrin's house in North Seattle, made a huge pot of decaf, and crowded around the dining table to confer.

"You'd think that my first ad spread in three years wouldn't create so damn much noise," Russell complained and Cassidy patted his shoulder in sympathy. "I should never have put my logo in the corner. I didn't put my name, just the damned logo. Designers are coming out of the woodwork looking for me. I got so effing tired of repeating that I'm retired and only do the work I initiate. So, I shut off my blasted phone and put a 'go away' auto-reply on my e-mail."

"My personal advice, Perrin," Jo's voice was definitely in her serious legal advice mode and they all stopped to listen. "Is duck and run. Don't stop until you and your family hit Tahiti at the very least." That got the laugh she was clearly aiming for. "How many hits did your website get again?"

"I stopped looking after the first five thousand," Perrin shuddered. "That was in the six hours after it hit the first newsstand.

Over a thousand of those were on the catalog request list. Russell, if I don't move to Tahiti, I'll need you to build me a catalog so that I can send it to them. Wait, Melanie, can I afford to print and mail that many catalogs?" She didn't pause for an answer. "Two hundred on the quote request list in the first hour. I'm so glad I never got an online store set up or I'd be so screwed."

Bill sat close with his arm wrapped loosely around his wife's narrow shoulders. Good man.

Melanie glanced at Joshua and knew he would react the same way if the crisis was landing on her shoulders.

"First," Melanie decided it was time to take some control. "First we have to stop and say congratulations to Perrin. Yes, you have just traded up for the next set of problems, but they are great problems to have."

"Why am I not feeling so lucky?"

"Because you're a very smart woman," Jo chimed in.

"You will," Melanie corrected Jo who actually winked at her. "Wait until the shock is over."

"Does that happen any time soon?" Perrin sounded very doubtful.

"*Non*," Melanie reassured her and got another laugh. "Second, if you ignore everything for a week or a month, it will not matter. All it will do is make you more mysterious. Zoran has turned mysterious into an art form. One of America's top fashion designers for the last three decades and he does not show up in Wikipedia except on the French site. He doesn't do runway shows or give interviews."

"But she has to fix it sometime, right?" Jaspar spoke up from where he sat close beside his sister. "Tam still gets to make her new clothes? I don't care about that girly stuff, but she does. Can she get a fashion spread like you, Mom?"

Calling her Mom clearly struck Perrin like a slap; a really good one that snapped her out of panic and back into thinking.

She leaned over to hug both her kids. "Tamara still gets her new line whenever she's ready. Even if we run away to Tahiti. I promise."

Melanie kept an eye on Jaspar. Perrin had totally melted at being called "Mom." Almost as if it was the first time. Just how smart was the boy, maybe sensing how much she needed encouragement at the moment? Or more likely, just feeling some connection and responding to it? His frank look back when he noticed Melanie's attention told her that it was the former and he just might be that insightful about people.

Had she been that smart at ten? No. She'd still been a naïve little girl. She'd certainly been that smart by the time she was eleven though, living in a car with her dangerously unpredictable mother.

"We need to come up with a plan for you to expand sooner than expected, but still not outstrip your income or your sanity."

"I'm glad to give you a loan, Perrin," Russell offered. "You know that. Whatever you need." The advantages of having a multi-millionaire in the room. Actually two of them. Melanie might not have Russell's immense family wealth, but she too could lay down some serious money if necessary.

"No," Perrin held up both hands. "No loans. I don't want to be beholden to anyone. This is my business. If I fail, fine. But I don't want something I might not be able to repay."

"Shit, Perrin, you know I wouldn't miss—"

"No," Melanie cut him off. "She's right. Different people make different decisions. Perrin needs to trust herself on this."

Bill and Perrin both reacted to that one by holding each other tighter. Melanie didn't know why what she'd said was important, but she could see the two of them becoming more solid, more supportive of each other in that moment.

What was it that Joshua had said? She inspired him. Well, he grounded her. Just as she could see what Bill and Perrin did for each other, Joshua grounded her more deeply in who she really was.

They all jumped when the doorbell rang, Perrin crying out in surprise.

Jo's dry voice was barely louder than Bill's footsteps crossing to the door with Joshua close behind in support. "Told you to run while you still had the chance."

AT THE FRONT DOOR, Angelo was waiting with a large thermal bag and several cloth carry sacks.

"Candygram!" he called out as soon as he spotted Bill and Josh.

Josh snorted out a laugh. Bill looked at them like they were both nuts.

Josh exchanged a look with Angelo. Next time they had a boys' night, it was definitely going to include a screening of *Blazing Saddles.*

They helped Angelo lug his care packages to the kitchen. As they passed through the dining room, Angelo repeated his call. Russell barked out a laugh; most of the women just rolled their eyes.

"What have you got here, Angelo?" Josh carried the heavy carriers into the kitchen.

"I figured you needed some sustenance. As soon as the dinner crowd was fed, I dropped the rest of the night on my new sous chef. Graziella is going to tell me how he does. Manuel has the other restaurant under control."

While Angelo and Bill distributed plates and uncovered platters of food, Josh uncorked a red and a white and circled the table pouring glasses. He dropped a bottle of sparkling cider between the kids. Perrin opened that and served them.

Angelo and Bill delivered a lasagna and a pan of Chicken Marsala to the table.

When Josh asked Perrin which she wanted she said quietly, "No wine. I'm fine with cider."

Something happened around the table. The guys didn't react, but the women sure did. An itchy feeling between Josh's shoulders had him grabbing Bill's shoulder before he could return to the kitchen.

"What?" Bill asked him.

"Not sure. Give it a moment," then he turned back to watch what was going on.

Jo and Cassidy had turned to Perrin, then Jo's eyes shot wide. Angelo continued around the table to Melanie. She was about to help him set down a plate in the center of the table, but it was as if she was moving in slow motion.

"I've got it," she told Angelo. But Josh could see that was the outer poise of the supermodel speaking. Inside, he saw the woman was also looking at Perrin with intense interest.

"Bill," Josh said softly. "I think you need to talk to your wife. Maybe out on the deck."

Perrin's fair skin, even lighter than Melanie's, blushed bright red at his words. "No. No, I think it should be here. In front of the children, in front of our friends."

"You okay, honey?" Bill moved up close, suddenly solicitous and filled with worry.

Josh was going to retreat to give them space, but figured maybe he'd better stay in case someone had to catch the man as he fell.

Perrin's laugh was bright and sharp. She was crying, but her smile was huge. "Am I okay? No! In so many ways." Again the over-bright laugh. "But in one way, really, really good. You know how we decided to try for one more kid right away?" Perrin shrugged. "It worked. The test this morning was positive."

"But we only just started last…" Bill trailed off.

Josh counted three seconds of dead silence before the man swept his wife off her chair and into his arms.

The room exploded with applause. Apparently the kids were fully on board with the plan of getting a younger brother or sister; they leapt into their parents' arms. Somewhere around their feet, a small dog who had been sleeping quietly in her dog bed began to yap until it too was scooped up to where it could lick someone's face.

Josh looked at Melanie. She was in profile to him. Somehow he and Constance had never reproduced. "Someday soon, first our careers." But someday had always been *soon*, never *now*. Looking at Melanie, Josh could easily imagine her with children. The lords above and below help him, but he could picture her with *their* children.

But there was no magic moment. No turn and locking of eyes. No instant silent awareness, as he would have written this scene. Instead Melanie was looking intently across the table.

Josh followed her gaze to Cassidy, who had gone sheet white. He couldn't make sense of why she was upset by what was clearly an incredibly happy and welcome event.

Melanie was up and moving and Josh circled the other way to back her up for whatever explosion was coming.

It wasn't an explosion. He arrived just in time to hear a desperate whisper.

"The date? What's the damned date?"

Melanie placed a hand on her shoulder and told her.

Cassidy began swearing softly, at least at first. It built rapidly into, "Goddamn you, Russell. I'm not ready for this. I'm so not ready."

Melanie tapped Russell on the shoulder to get his attention.

"What? Hey, you okay, babe? You need some wine?"

"No." Cassidy's voice was abruptly sharp and loud enough to silence the room. "No. I don't want any God. Damn. *Wine*."

"What, honey?" Russell brushed Melanie aside as he gathered his wife to her feet and tried to hug her. She shoved him back until they stood a half-foot apart, she glaring up at her much taller husband. Now everyone was on their feet around the table watching.

Josh still didn't have any idea what was going on.

"That night," she snarled up at Russell.

"Could you be more specific?"

"Just how much did we have to drink that night?"

"What night? Oh. I had a fair bit and I think you had… Wait… Just hold on." Now it was Russell's turn to go sheet white.

Josh didn't have it yet, but he was close. Melanie rolled her eyes at him, then momentarily rested her head on her own shoulder as if sleeping. As if sleeping on her own…no, on *his* shoulder.

He and Melanie had too much to drink and slept together without sex. Russell and Cassidy had the sex that night, but hadn't used any— Oh.

Cassidy gave a long-suffering sigh and leaned her forehead against her husband's chest. Russell automatically wrapped his arms around her. A moment later he stepped her back and looked down into her face.

"Really?"

"I'm late. You know I'm never late."

"Really?"

"Russell!" she ground out his name between clenched teeth. "Could you say something more useful than: really?"

"Holy shit! Really?"

She laughed and leaned back in against his chest. He scooped her up and sank back into his chair with her now cradled in his lap.

Josh pulled Melanie close so that he could slip a hand around her waist.

"Anyone else?" Cassidy's comment had just a touch of snide irritation, but Josh wasn't buying it as she delivered it from where she sat in Russell's lap.

Melanie held up her hands palm out.

Jo shook her head, but the look she sent Angelo told Josh that they might start trying very soon.

He and Melanie returned to the kitchen to take over the last of the unloading.

"Is that one of your future scenes in our story, Joshua?"

He took the time to kiss her slowly and thoroughly, the food could wait a minute. "Yes. A child with you? Very much yes. Not a deal breaker, but—"

Her smile answered him, "Too many words, Joshua. But I agree. If we can figure this out, that is definitely part of our story. I think just one. But yes."

There simply had to be a way to make this work.

"Maria should be here. And Hogan."

She was right. At his nod of agreement, Melanie pulled out her phone and called them. Asked if they could come right away, they needed more advice about how to handle the business success.

"You are so cruel," he teased her. "You didn't tell them."

"And have them race needlessly? And ruin the surprise? *Non!* That is not for me to do."

Josh knew only one way to answer that, "You better-than-perfect woman you." He kissed her quickly and carried the last of the food to the table.

Dinner was about half eaten when Maria and Hogan arrived. Once again, the mayhem was complete.

MELANIE KNEW they had to return to the problem of Perrin's looming success or Perrin would be awake half the night and be overwhelmed by what was sure to begin happening tomorrow, no matter how they tried to ignore it.

When the dinner was done, she got the kids organized to clear everything off the table and into the kitchen. The table was far smaller than the monster in Maria's condo, but they all managed to crowd together as they once again faced the problem that had brought them there in the first place.

Melanie spoke first. "There are things you can accelerate. The expansion of your sewing space and staff is the most critical. I can help you do that this week. And Russell knows contractors better than most. You may not want his money, but you should accept his advice and help."

Perrin nodded stiffly. It was passive, the shock of the news and the child enough to overload anyone's brain. At least tonight she'd understand that there were viable solutions, even if she couldn't remember them in the morning.

"The biggest problem is how to protect you. You are a business owner and a designer. Never, ever make the mistake Donna did. You are not to be the CEO. You need someone to run the business for you."

"Raquel?" So, Perrin was still listening and thinking.

"No. She runs your storefront. She'd be overwhelmed. With this kind of exposure, you need a high-level manager as soon as you can afford one. Before then. Maybe you could get someone by offering them a share of the business instead of a salary at first."

Russell tossed out a couple names from the New York fashion industry.

"Georg retired since you came west," Melanie began ticking them off on her fingers. "He owns a fishing boat down in Florida. Kenalla and Perrin would kill each other in a week. It turns out that the reason Perrin got the ad placement she did was because your third suggestion is now in jail for embezzlement. He was caught trying to board a plane for Argentina. The company isn't even bankrupt, it was a shell that he gutted and overnight it is simply gone."

"And why do I want one of these people?" Perrin was back. Leaning forward, thinking. It was right. This was her business after all.

"You don't," Joshua cut off Melanie's reply.

Melanie turned to him. "Yes she does, Joshua. She can't do this herself."

"No. She doesn't want one of *those* people."

"I do know more about this than—"

He held up a hand to silence her. It was a commanding, peremptory gesture she'd never expect from him.

"Can we talk in private for a moment?"

Talk? He wanted to talk when he was obviously so wrong. When... No. Maybe he was trying to take their first fight out of the room.

She almost told him to go to hell.

"Please?" His whisper was a soft caress. She didn't like that he had that much power over her, to change her mood with so simple an action. But she couldn't deny the sincerity of his request.

"No!" Perrin called out as Melanie started to rise. "Look. This is family. Cassidy and I, we did our thing in front of everybody. So just do it here. We're *all* family."

Melanie would have flinched, but it used to give her mother too much satisfaction; Melanie had trained herself out of it. Family? Apparently not. She'd begun to think there was a way for her and Joshua to be family, but she'd been right all along. Family was toxic.

"Give us a break, Perrin. It's personal," Joshua kept his tone light, cajoling. Is that what he'd been doing to her? Manipulating her with kindness?

"Oh? And finding out you're pregnant isn't personal?" Cassidy shot out a second salvo. "Just try it, Josh. My whole world just changed." Then her look went impossibly soft and she turned to plant a kiss on Russell's cheek. "Oh man did it ever change."

"She's right, Josh. Melanie." Russell pointed a finger at their chairs. "Sit your asses down and lay it out on the table. This is family. All of this." He looked directly at Melanie on that last statement.

It was a look she recognized, one he'd been unable to give her years ago. Whatever else Russell might feel for his wife, he had found enough love in his heart that he also loved Melanie. She couldn't walk away from that.

She settled into her chair.

"Do it up, Josh," Russell shifted his gaze. "Whatever it is, spit it out."

Joshua looked at her uncertainly. Then turned to look around the table.

Melanie followed his gaze.

Bill with Perrin pulled so close they were practically in the same chair, their children leaning on their dad's shoulders. Maria and Hogan holding hands as were Jo and Angelo. Cassidy still sitting in Russell's lap with his big arms keeping her safe.

And Joshua.

Melanie folded her hands in her lap and stilled them. She was ready now. Her shields were back in place, at least mostly. No one here would see her reactions. No one except Joshua from whom she'd never been able to hide the slightest emotion.

He clearly read her irritation and her tightly held composure, offering a short apologetic nod that he'd made her feel that way.

Well, she wasn't going to start. There was not the least chase she would be making it any easier for him. Again he acknowledged her choice and began speaking.

"The reason I wanted to talk in private," he offered a scowl to the others around the table.

Out of the corner of her eye she could see Perrin stick her tongue out at him. Melanie wanted to cheer.

"The reason was, I need to preface my question with the fact that I love you—"

"Duh!" "We knew that." "That's all?"

They both ignored the others' comments. Joshua waited for them to die down. Melanie wondered if hope or horror was going to follow that statement. This was Joshua, she really, really wanted it to be hope.

She nodded for him to continue, offering him a slight smile of encouragement, as much as she dared.

His shoulders eased, a tiny bit, before he continued.

"And I wanted you to know that my idea, my question, if you are willing, is motivated only in thinking about what might be best for you and Perrin. It also could work in our, uh, novel project, but—"

"No codes!" "Cheater! Cheater! Pumpkin eater!"

"Okay!" Joshua turned on the table with a snarl jolted the others into silence and caused her to lean back as well.

She'd never seen or heard Joshua be openly angry. He'd clearly been livid when she'd revealed the story of her past, but that had been other-direct. This was completely different. She hadn't known he was capable of showing fury. It was a dark, fierce sound that commanded silence and attention.

"No codes? Fine. I'll give you no codes. I'm trying to figure out how to spend the rest of my life with this woman without doing to her what her bitch mother did. I don't want to force her to be even the least bit different than she truly is because she is so perfectly herself and I wouldn't change her for all the world. I love her so much that I'll just die if she walks away. Is that clear enough for you all?"

Melanie's gasp was the only sound around the perfectly still table. Thank God! She had misread Joshua. She was only slowly getting better at trust, and he'd know that about her, too. How perfectly he understood her. Angry *for* her, not at her.

Apparently satisfied with the results of his tirade, he turned back to her. It was so quiet that her ears actually rang.

"I have an idea," his voice was impossibly back to a caress that she could now appreciate. "It's about your career. It would also be good for us, I really think it would. But I don't want that to influence your decision at all. I'll follow you, or be at home waiting for you when you get back. I don't care, I just want to be with you."

She nodded carefully for him to continue.

Then he began to lay out his plan.

CHAPTER 17

The Smashing Six had gathered at Perrin's store to get dressed up before going out to dinner. Tamara was almost a-dither as much as Perrin over her inclusion in a girls' night out.

They'd coaxed Cassidy into a flowing dress of tropical fabrics which clung and revealed with every move she made. Jo had struggled against her fashion fate, but a cocktail dress of sky-blue jersey had revealed quite how impressive her voluptuous figure really was. Tamara wore the first of her own designs which was both edgy and inventive.

"Your turn," Perrin announced merrily.

Melanie had turned for the racks. There was a suit of dark blue she'd been itching to try, but Perrin simply shook her head and led her into the back, commanding the others to find something out front for Maria. Only Perrin and Tamara went into the back design studio with her.

The renovation had been completed in just two weeks. A door had been punched through into the larger space beyond. The area now smelled of fresh paint and new equipment. The first five stations were set up in the efficient sewing room that could hold at least five more. Karissa, Clem, and the newly hired Celine would be starting in there tomorrow.

Melanie could only marvel at the changes that had been wrought, both in Perrin's shop and in herself. She remembered those first days, sitting here, knowing she didn't belong but having nowhere else to go.

Just a month-and-a-half later and she felt completely at home amid the whirl of conversations. Now it was familiar and welcoming. She loved being here.

At Perrin's command, Melanie's closed her eyes.

"But Perrin—"

"But Melanie!" she responded. "No peeking!"

She huffed out her exasperation, but closed her eyes.

She could tell the instant the cloth touched her skin. This was her dress. Nothing felt like fifty-dollar a yard satin. It wrapped, caressed. Perrin had built in support, so only the scantiest of panties separated her from pure unadulterated heaven.

Even if she'd have less reason to wear such things in public now, maybe she would model it for Joshua. If he were a good boy. And he was. A *exceptionally* good boy.

His grand plan was so simple, she still marveled that she hadn't seen it herself. She could still take the occasional modeling job, if she was in the mood. But she had something far more interesting to do now.

Perrin and Tamara fussed around her, reminding her every thirty seconds to keep her eyes closed until she'd almost wanted to snap at them. When Tamara tied a swatch of heavy corduroy over her eyes, it was a relief. Few designers minded her seeing the dress before the tweaks of a final fitting, but Perrin had been so insistent.

Her cell phone rang somewhere. The ring said it was her business line. A groping hand, someone placed it into her palm. She answered it blind.

"This is Melanie."

"Oh, I'm so glad I caught you."

"Hi, Sue. How is the shoot going?" It was easier to be civil now about missing the swimsuit issue. The passing month had helped as well.

"That's why I called. I don't know how to do this properly, so I'll just blurt it out. I need you."

Melanie remained stone silent. She didn't know how to react, she honestly didn't. Sue took that as an opening.

"That new girl we brought on; I can't even say her name I'm so upset. She's currently the cover shot—"

"Congratulate her for me." It took everything in her power to not end the call, to not say something snide and burn the bridge once and for all. Sue continued as if Melanie hadn't spoken.

"—in the London papers: *News of the World* and *The Sun*. It will be hitting the U.S. tabloids by the weekend. The little bitch was selling lap dances in one of those Russian discos. There were paparazzi shots; she was wearing nothing but one of *our* bathing suits that she kept when she stayed behind after the shoot. She wasn't drunk or stoned—not a single decent excuse I could use in the press—just a wild little bitch. Took money, let them… Let's just say I've seen streetwalkers with more class. I need you. I need the Melanie magic to offset this news. We go to press incredibly soon. We're in final photo selection right now and just had to throw away half of our 'Moscow in the Spring' collection, damn that place is so cold. Please, please, please. I saw that hot-hot spread you had in *Fashion Alive* and was just kicking myself. And now this. You have to save me. I'll grovel. Anything you want."

Actually, she thought that Sue was doing a pretty impressive grovel already. Melanie's brain kicked into high gear. She wanted this. Not like she had before, but she wanted this to prove that she still had it. Was still in the game.

Shove that aside. Think like a businesswoman. No. More than that.

"Hang on, Sue." She muted the phone.

"Perrin," Melanie called out into the darkness of her blindfolded eyes.

"Yes?" She was so close they were almost touching.

"Do you do any swimwear? Really sexy, short-out-a-man's-brain kind of swimwear?"

"Some. On you? Oh yeah. It would be screamingly hot. I did fluorescents this year, amazing with your hair and skin tone. And I can make more. I have the materials right here and more ideas already sketched that I just haven't had time to build. Tammy also did a couple knitwear coverups that aren't that vibe but would look really good on you, too."

There was a bright squeak from Tammy that sounded as if she cut it off by slapping both hands over her mouth.

Melanie considered the factors. "Do you want to skip three or four levels at once and trade up for a whole different set of problems?"

"You're the CEO. You tell me." Melanie could hear Perrin's smile.

That had been Joshua's elegant solution. Melanie would step in as CEO. She had the knowledge and the equally necessary industry clout. She'd also save the startup corporation, Perrin's Glorious Garb, a small fortune of money while guaranteeing international-quality presentation by being its signature model as well. She'd get to take Perrin global, and still do the modeling she so loved.

Melanie clicked the phone back off mute, "You still there, Sue?"

"Right here."

"Okay. Here are my conditions. If you say yes, we can deliver the images within seventy-two hours. Condition one: I will be using Pike Place Market and a fine Italian restaurant as my locations. Maybe throw in a Seattle ferry for a Northwesty bonus."

That should boost Jo and Angelo's national profile significantly. And she'd bet she could talk Joshua into another ferry ride, especially if she was clad only in Perrin's swimwear.

"We can fly you there," Sue sounded eager.

"I am in Seattle right now, along with my second condition: I will have Russell Morgan do the shoot."

"Oh yes. Russell's amazing. I can't believe you found him. Seattle? Really? That's where he went? Whatever for? Never mind. Don't care. Yes and yes so far."

"I knew you'd like that. Third and final: I will be exclusively providing all of the swimwear, each piece of which will have the standard designer credit. Trust me, it will be innovative." Melanie knew that sight unseen because Perrin didn't know how to design anything that wasn't.

"Done. Contract within the hour."

"Standard rates plus my and Russell's rush fees."

"Okay," she gave a very insincere sigh about the rush fee, but she had to know that was coming. "You're the best, Melanie. By the way…"

"Yes?"

"We haven't selected the cover yet."

Melanie did her best to keep the smile out of her voice, "Always a pleasure doing business, Sue."

She hung up and held the phone out into the darkness. It was taken from her fingers.

"Holy shit!" Perrin breathed out slowly from where she'd apparently been frozen close by Melanie's side. "Did you just get into the swimsuit issue with my clothes?"

Tamara's squeal of excitement was loud enough that Melanie could hear all the others rushing into the back studio.

As Tamara cried out the news, there were numerous gasps

and comments, some of which made sense and some of which didn't. The latter included a fair amount of shushing noises.

Melanie was still blindfolded and couldn't see their expressions to figure out what was going on.

"Can we lose the blindfold, Perrin? Please? Anyway, Lesson One in business: never burn a bridge." Joshua and his counting lists were rubbing off on her. "Lesson Two in business: there's no longer a me, there's only an us."

"Well, you may think that, Melanie, but you're wrong."

"Oh?" she tried to sound arch and haughty, but there was a merriness to Perrin's tone that made her attempt a total failure. The others were laughing as well.

Fingers worked at the loose knot of her blindfold.

"Sometimes," Perrin whispered in her ear over the noise in the room, "it *is* all about you."

And she slid the blindfold aside.

Melanie stood in front of a three-fold modeling mirror.

But it was a Melanie she barely recognized.

The bright sheen of the pearly Duchesse satin shimmered down her length like water. The strapless bodice was an elegant finger weave of the Duchesse and the palest sky blue of the crepe back satin. The slightest breath caused the satins to shift and shimmer, all the more apparent because of the contrast of the shiny and the crepe textures. The blue brought her eyes to light like sapphires without the hardness that some blues caused. Bright and soft.

The sheen of the dress had been complemented by a lacy, pearl-studded, flowing back veil that left her face exposed and, while covering her hair, still allowed it to spread and billow. It positively shone.

"*Mariée!*" Even to herself her voice sounded drifty with wonder. "A bride! You made me a wedding dress, Perrin. All this time, you were making me a wedding dress."

Perrin moved up beside her in the mirror and reached out to tweak a seam.

Melanie brushed her hand aside and then grabbed it and held on. "You don't mess with something this perfect. I can't wait to wear this for Joshua."

"Not before the wedding!" they all chimed in unison, and gathered close around to look at her in the mirror.

"Of course not. He hasn't even proposed yet. I won't let him. We both agree it is too soon." She turned in profile, unable to believe what she was seeing. In an entire career built on looking beautiful, she had never looked this *magnifique* before. Not even close. "But I can't wait."

"Oh, I got you an early wedding present. Maria and Angelo are giving you the condo—"

"Perrin!" Maria and Jo cut her off.

"Crap! I wasn't supposed to say that. You didn't hear that. But they are. This isn't nearly that impressive."

Perrin handed her a small card.

Melanie first gave Maria and Jo a hug.

The condo. It was so perfect for them. A gift she couldn't accept. She'd buy it. Though she'd insist on that later. That wasn't a problem.

It was a home.

A real home, with Joshua. They'd make the second bedroom into an office for him. Or perhaps convert the overlarge pantry just off the kitchen he so enjoyed cooking in. Then the bedroom could be for a child.

She had to blink aside the tears that threatened to overwhelm her. The circle of friends, *The Smashing Six*. These were the women she would have as lifelong friends. Have children with. Grow old with.

A family.

The word, which had gutted Melanie for her whole life, was now a gift beyond price.

She had to wipe away more tears before she could read the card.

Perrin's Glorious Garb. Her name and title: CEO.

CEO. The card made it real. She'd found her back door. Except it wasn't some safety net to the end of her real career. Instead it said that her entire career to date had only been building toward this new beginning.

She hugged Perrin, carefully so as not to muss the dress.

Perrin was looking at her strangely, "Read it again. Out loud."

"Perrin's Glorious Garb. Melanie *Harper*." She didn't manage to get the title out past the sudden tightness in her throat.

It took her a moment, and then it wrapped around her like lover's embrace.

Years ago she'd thrown away a last name that meant nothing.

And now she'd have the name that meant everything.

And always would.

KEEP READING

Keep reading for an excerpt from book #6,
a five-story collection:
Where Dreams Continue
And reviews are a HUGE help.
Thanks for joining my journey, Matt.

IF YOU ENJOYED THIS, YOU MIGHT
ALSO ENJOY:

WHERE DREAMS CONTINUE
(EXCERPT)

STARTING WITH: WHERE DREAMS TASTE
LIKE CHOCOLATE

"*M*adonna Mother of God!" Tony Bosco would have had the crown of his head smacked with a wooden spoon by Grandma for saying it, but he couldn't help himself.

His cousin Vic looked up from where he'd been sliding the latest tray of dark chocolate orange truffles into the display case. Together they stared out the large plate-glass window that faced onto the Madison Street sidewalk, at the east edge of Seattle.

"Oh, yes. She is something, isn't she?"

Something? Tony couldn't even speak. He hadn't prayed in years but he wanted to drop to his knees on the linoleum and beg God himself to make her turn in at their chocolate shop's door. He'd been back in Seattle for only three hours and he had just seen a goddess—unlike any woman he'd found in his entire five years in Europe.

When she did indeed turn toward him, he considered maybe Grandma was right and he should start going back to church.

With a bright tinkle of the bells on the back of the door, she breezed in. Five-ten of statuesque redhead in a flirty dress—the

shade of beaten copper that clung to her like a dusting of sugar
—strolled into the shop. The calf-high boots and accompanying
short hem on the dress didn't *imply* a thing; the combo shouted,
"Amazing legs!"

"I need two of your finest, Vic. It's a beautiful Friday."

Tony couldn't have said it better himself.

Vic already had a pair of his ginger caramel dark chocolates
in a tiny sack. He exchanged them for the six dollars she already
had out in her hand, her long graceful hand.

With a cheery, *"Ciao!"* she was gone out the door and Tony
was left listening to the ringing bell rather than that silky voice,
American English, but seasoned with Italian. Gone so fast he
didn't even have an eye color for her, though an impression of
bright blue existed somewhere in his head.

"What the hell was that?" He still didn't have his breath back.

Vic laughed, "Don't worry. You'll never get used to her. But
every Friday, if she's had a good week, she comes and buys two
dark chocolate ginger caramels. Won't buy anything else, so I
make sure to never run out on a Friday."

"And if she's had a bad week?"

"Don't see her, but thankfully that doesn't happen so much. I
do so look forward to these days."

"Couldn't you have, like, slowed her down for a moment?"
Tony knew he hadn't blinked, and still there hadn't been a
chance to look at her clearly. Too many first impressions and
too little time to sort through them. He sniffed the air, but could
find not one hint of her. Only the rich smell of fine chocolate
remained in the shop.

"Can't be done."

"Because you haven't tried."

"Tried plenty, Cuz. Not happening."

Tony rolled his eyes at his cousin. Vic had always been a lame-
ass when it came to meeting girls. Actually, he'd been stellar at it,

as long as Tony wasn't around. Tony always managed first choice, which he never complained about and only lorded over his cousin at every *other* opportunity, not wanting to be too obnoxious.

His cousin laughed at him, "Okay, Mr. Hotshot European Chocolatier. Next week, I'll keep my big mouth shut, you go ahead and try. Not a thing on this planet is gonna slow that woman down."

He didn't want her to slow down, he certainly never did that himself. He just wanted to move down the same path for a length or two, long enough for a wild affair. Tony turned back to the chocolate-making work counter and looked down at what Vic had given him on his return to the States just hours before.

His cousin had taken over the shop and the family recipes when their shared grandparents had retired and gone RVing. He'd never thought they were the sort, impossible to imagine them *not* in this shop. But they were off to tour every scenic byway in the country.

He'd never really thought he'd be back here. He'd worked in some of Europe's premier chocolateries, been trained by master chefs, but the old shop felt comfortable. It was the right size. A cozy front area for customers to stare into the large glass display cases, small enough for a friendly jostling of elbows as they picked and chose, but not cramped or crowded. The kitchen was behind, with no door to hide it away from the curious who wanted to peek over the cabinets. Light streamed in, bright through the front glass, dappled by trees through the high, kitchen windows in back.

This shop is where the two boys had spent every summer as kids. Once Vic had taken over, he'd increased business to the point where he could either manage the shop or make the chocolates, but not both. Seattle loved chocolate treats, and had plenty of companies catering to that craving. But even with competition, Granddad's recipes were making a name for The Chocolaterie Bosco.

Tony had been at his usual loose ends when Vic called. He'd been hanging in Milan where his latest girlfriend had dumped him. Normally it worked the other way, but when the captain of the winning Italian team of the Tour de France swept her up, he knew he'd been totally outclassed. They'd been close to done anyway.

Il Cioccolato Bello only needed him for pick up work. He'd learned all he was going to at Oui Chocolat in Chartres outside of Paris. He'd plumbed the depths of Die Schokolade Maestro in Hamburg. And even thinking of the head chocolatiers at Kāko in New Zealand or Callebaut in Belgium made him exhausted, he was so not excited about "going back to school."

So, Vic had given him an excuse to move once more half around the world and come make chocolate for a small but enthusiastic clientele. Just the two of them and a part-time clerk on the weekend, closed Mondays and Tuesdays.

He leaned on the work counter and stared down at the dozens of hand-scribed index cards laid out across the cool marble slab. Vic had set them out for him. Granddad's sloppy handwriting was faded on some to near illegibility, partially lost behind chocolate smears on others, but there was a voice here. A voice Tony had seen and loved, but perhaps never really heard.

He picked up one that he thought might entice *la belle signora*.

"I'll start here," he held up the card.

"Courvoisier-brandied cherry," Vic nodded his approval. They shared a smile. They both remembered the trouble they'd earned for dropping a pair of them down the back of Vic's older sister's dress one summer then smacking them so that they burst, just moments before her date arrived. The long red stains had never come out and they'd both learned an appreciation—

over many, many tedious unpaid hours of manual labor at the shop—just how much fine girl clothes cost.

Keep reading.
Available at fine retailers everywhere:
Where Dreams Continue

ABOUT THE AUTHOR

USA Today and Amazon #1 Bestseller M. L. "Matt" Buchman has 70+ contemporary and military romance novels, and action-adventure thrillers. Also 100 short stories and lotsa audiobooks.

Booklist says: 3x "Top 10 Romance of the Year" and among "The 20 Best Romantic Suspense Novels: Modern Master-pieces." NPR and B&N say: "Best 5 Romance of the Year." PW declares: "Tom Clancy fans open to a strong female lead will clamor for more."

A project manager with a geophysics degree, he's designed and built houses, flown and jumped out of planes, solo-sailed a 50' sailboat, and bicycled solo around the world...and he quilts. More at: www.mlbuchman.com.

Other works by M. L. Buchman: *(* - also in audio)*

Action-Adventure Thrillers

Dead Chef
One Chef!
Two Chef!

Miranda Chase
Drone*
Thunderbolt*
Condor*
Ghostrider*
Raider*
Chinook*
Havoc*
White Top*

Romantic Suspense

Delta Force
Target Engaged*
Heart Strike*
Wild Justice*
Midnight Trust*

Firehawks
MAIN FLIGHT
Pure Heat
Full Blaze
Hot Point*
Flash of Fire*
Wild Fire

SMOKEJUMPERS
Wildfire at Dawn*
Wildfire at Larch Creek*
Wildfire on the Skagit*

The Night Stalkers
MAIN FLIGHT
The Night Is Mine
I Own the Dawn
Wait Until Dark
Take Over at Midnight

Light Up the Night
Bring On the Dusk
By Break of Day
AND THE NAVY
Christmas at Steel Beach
Christmas at Peleliu Cove
WHITE HOUSE HOLIDAY
Daniel's Christmas*
Frank's Independence Day*
Peter's Christmas*
Zachary's Christmas*
Roy's Independence Day*
Damien's Christmas*
5E
Target of the Heart
Target Lock on Love
Target of Mine
Target of One's Own

Shadow Force: Psi
At the Slightest Sound*
At the Quietest Word*
At the Merest Glance*
At the Clearest Sensation*

White House Protection Force
Off the Leash*
On Your Mark*
In the Weeds*

Contemporary Romance

Eagle Cove
Return to Eagle Cove
Recipe for Eagle Cove
Longing for Eagle Cove
Keepsake for Eagle Cove

Henderson's Ranch
Nathan's Big Sky*
Big Sky, Loyal Heart*
Big Sky Dog Whisperer*

Other works by M. L. Buchman:

Contemporary Romance (cont)

Love Abroad
Heart of the Cotswolds: England
Path of Love: Cinque Terre, Italy

Where Dreams
Where Dreams are Born
Where Dreams Reside
*Where Dreams Are of Christmas**
Where Dreams Unfold
Where Dreams Are Written
Where Dreams Continue

Science Fiction / Fantasy

Deities Anonymous
Cookbook from Hell: Reheated
Saviors 101

Single Titles
The Nara Reaction
Monk's Maze
the Me and Elsie Chronicles

Non-Fiction

Strategies for Success
Managing Your Inner Artist/Writer
*Estate Planning for Authors**
Character Voice
*Narrate and Record Your Own Audiobook**

Short Story Series by M. L. Buchman:

Romantic Suspense

Antarctic Ice Fliers

Delta Force
Th Delta Force Shooters
The Delta Force Warriors

Firehawks
The Firehawks Lookouts
The Firehawks Hotshots
The Firebirds

The Night Stalkers
The Night Stalkers 5D Stories
The Night Stalkers 5E Stories
The Night Stalkers CSAR
The Night Stalkers Wedding Stories

US Coast Guard

White House Protection Force

Contemporary Romance

Eagle Cove

Henderson's Ranch*

Where Dreams

Action-Adventure Thrillers

Dead Chef

Miranda Chase Origin Stories

Science Fiction / Fantasy

Deities Anonymous

Other
The Future Night Stalkers
Single Titles

SIGN UP FOR M. L. BUCHMAN'S NEWSLETTER TODAY

and receive:
Release News
Free Short Stories
a Free Starter Anthology

Do it today. Do it now.
www.mlbuchman.com/newsletter

www.ingramcontent.com/pod-product-compliance
Lightning Source LLC
Chambersburg PA
CBHW020627110726
47899CB00002B/685